A SYMPHONY FOR NONE

A NOVEL EXPERIENCE

E.P. LANE

Edited by
PAUL MARTIN

For my wife Mooni:
I couldn't ask for a better friend.

CONTENTS

1
___

NO ONE TO PLAY WITH

"Hey, turn that up real quick."

"Now, I know this isn't what you usually hear on 104.3 Radio here in Rivers, but this song we're about to play now is a special case. After months of anticipation, Nowell Lewis and Brianne Green are moving to Rivers. Yes, the married couple, the iconic 90s soul duo, Lonely Souls. The two met in 1995 at the now-closed Neo Lounge. The couple married in 1996 and released their first album, Ataraxic, in 1997. The album was a sleeper hit and...well, I'll let the music speak for itself. Here's the first single from Lonely Souls, 'Limbless Ghosts.'"

    The king is fertile on a spring
    Morning; would he ever pen she as one to thieve?
    Little by little, rolling stones gather moss
    And share a heart tossed by two lions once feral.

    UNFURLING LOVE from the murks of minds.
    There is no code, no X marking the spot.
    No limbless ghosts, just our arms
    And legs longing to never be separate.

Nowell Lewis and Brianne Green decided to move to the small city of Rivers, USA with their 14-year-old son, Toby Lewis-Green, in the hopes of escaping mounting rumors of the married couple's past. While no one in the media seems to know the actual content of these rumors, Nowell and Brianne feel the pressure of a big secret revealing itself at any given moment. In an attempt to keep the low profile the family has held since the birth of their son in 2001, Nowell is now driving his family safely to the aforementioned Rivers. After asking his wife to turn up the radio upon passing a sign indicating that Rivers is only five miles out, Nowell is taken aback by hearing the results of one of his most fateful life decisions on the airwaves for the first time in years.

"God, I haven't actually *heard* this song in so long, Bri," Nowell says. "Our first single, gah, where does the time go?"

"We were so *into* ourselves back then," Brianne says with a smile on her face.

"You still are," Toby says from the backseat. Toby has become annoyed listening to his parent's incessant chatter about themselves during their car ride to Rivers, let alone living under the same roof as these people. "Dad, you actually asked Mom to turn up the radio for your *own* song?"

"If it wasn't for that song and many others," Nowell says, pointing at Toby by way of the rear-view mirror, "you wouldn't be here living the good life with us, Son. You've never had to worry about anything in your life--nor will you ever."

"I hardly call this the good life," Toby says. "You two are famous, and yet we move to Rivers. And why now? Because you guys are afraid of some rumors?"

Brianne turns from the front passenger seat to look at Toby, shades hiding her eyes. "Don't talk to anyone about those stupid rumors, Toby. They will only cause more trouble."

"What is there to talk about," Toby says. "I don't even know what they are, and *you* guys sure as hell won't talk about it."

"Language," Nowell says, his eyes focused on the road.

"Sorry," Toby says. "I don't understand."

"What's not to understand?" Brianne says, still looking at Toby.

"I don't...understand, Mom. *Anything* that's going on. Like the radio guy said, it's been three months, and I don't know what the fuss is about."

Focused on the road, Nowell says, "The fuss is that your mother and I know that it's long overdue for us to give back to the community."

"Why couldn't we give back to our community back home?" Toby says, leaning forward. Brianne turns back around in her seat to face the road. "Why here? In Rivers?"

"It's more meaningful to aid those that actually need help, Son," Nowell says. "You think our old community needs aid in any kind of way besides the latest way to boost their egos?" He scoffs. "That place is toxic," he says.

"It'll be good for us," Brianne says, leaning her head to the left. "We promise."

Toby leans back into the seat and sighs. "Okay."

Not long after their conversation, the family drives past the welcome sign for Rivers. After exiting off the interstate, Nowell creeps through downtown Rivers to reach his family's new home, frequently glancing at his GPS to make sure he doesn't make a single wrong turn. During the drive, Toby looks through the back passenger window to observe Rivers for the first time. The closer the family gets to their house, the less interesting Rivers becomes. Toby makes note of a movie theater, several fast-food restaurants, a performing arts theater, car dealerships, several Mexican food restaurants, and one too many gas stations, but hardly any residents.

"I thought you guys said this place was small?" Toby asks, astounded by his available options in the small city.

"Small for us," Nowell says through a yawn. "Trust me, Son, in a few days you'll be suffocating."

Toby is already suffocating. The smaller scope than what he is accustomed to simply caught him off guard. Rivers is a city that Toby believes he can become intimate with, waiting to have every alley explored, every showing at either theater experienced, and every dish, domestic or foreign, examined.

The family pulls up to their new home.

"We have arrived," Brianne says with a smile on her face. Nowell turns the car off, and the family gets out of the car. Toby looks at his home from the driveway. 5000 square feet of his parent's wealth standing wide and high in its eggshell-white glory. Toby couldn't have been more shocked that his parents would choose to stay at a mansion in a small city they claimed to want to help. This gesture, to move here in Rivers only to still live in their own form of luxury, only made the line between love and contempt for his parents blurrier for Toby.

"What do you think, Toby?" Brianne asks, twirling around to face him after they all close their car doors.

Toby, being on the passenger side with his mother, looks straight at her and says, "Thank you, guys. You've really outdone yourselves."

"Of course, we did," Brianne says, still smiling. She turns around, puts her shades away, and walks toward the house.

"Naturally, all your stuff is inside and organized in a way that both your father and I believe you will see fit."

Toby and Nowell walk toward their new home, as well. "You and Dad told me you sold most of my stuff."

"That was a joke, Son," Nowell says. "I still can't believe you think we're so cruel."

"You said this place was small."

The family go inside their home and stand in front of the steps that lead upstairs.

Brianne sighs in relief. "It's good to finally be home. Nowell, can you go to the car and bring our things in?"

Nowell takes a step closer to Brianne, puts his right hand on her back, and gives her a kiss on the cheek. "Sure thing, dear." He exits through the front doors, leaving them both open.

Brianne looks at Toby. "So," she says, looking at him inquiringly, "what did you think about Rivers while we were driving through?"

Toby shrugs and walks over to an end table, half-observing a lamp. "It seems okay." He looks at his mother. "There were hardly any people out. It was kind of weird."

"Oh, well that's because it's a college town, sweetheart," Brianne says with a wave of her hand. She walks toward Toby, heels echoing from the wooden floor, grabbing his hand away from the lamp and holding it. "It's the beginning of May, so a lot of the people that live here are slowly moving back home to their families and finishing their classes online."

"So, it's not usually this empty?"

Brianne smiles. "No, sweetie." She quickly rubs Toby's hair with her other hand. "Just during vacation times. You know, summer, Christmas, things like that. Are you worried about making new friends?" She places the hand she rubbed his hair with on his arm.

"Not really."

Brianne steps back and puts her hands together to her face as if praying. "How about you walk around town and look for some people your age?"

"I should probably help you and Dad get settled, don't you think, Mom?"

"Oh no," Brianne says, hands in her pockets now. "Your father and I will be fine." She grabs Toby by his arm and drags him out the front door, Toby protesting along the way. "Go on," Brianne continues. "Go see what the youth of Rivers is all about. Just be back for dinner."

"What are we having?"

"You'll have to be here to see," Brianne says, winking.

With that, Toby is sent out into the small city of Rivers alone. Despite the occasional breeze, Toby quickly finds that walking through Rivers is exhausting as the heat beats down on the pavement. After about an hour of walking, Toby decides to visit a gas station to get a drink. He walks past a group of four teenagers sitting by the doors, one of whom nods at him, and goes inside. Toby grabs the biggest bottle of water he can find, walks up to the register, and pays. After exiting the door, he stands by the teenagers, opens the bottle, and takes huge gulps. One of the teens, a red-haired boy, looks up at him, laughing.

"That bad, huh?"

Toby abruptly stops lapping down his water to answer, but he chokes, getting water everywhere. The teenagers laugh at him, the closest one, a black boy, getting in a brown-haired boy's lap to avoid getting water on him.

"Do we need to teach you how to drink water, kid?" the red-haired boy asks.

"Or to talk, perhaps," the black boy adds.

"No," Toby says between struggling coughs. "No, thank you, I'm fine."

"Alrighty," the red-haired boy says. He looks at the black boy. "Hey, Eric, get out of Chris's lap, why don't you."

"Sorry," Eric says, getting out of the boy's lap. "Trying not to melt."

"I think our friend here with the water has melted enough for the four of us," a blonde girl says from the end of the row. The red-haired boy has his left arm around her. She looks up at Toby. "Are you okay, by the way?"

Toby, mostly composed now, says, "Yeah, thank you," before coughing again. He sits down by Eric and clears his throat. He looks to his left to face the four teenagers. "My name's Toby, by the way." He extends his hand for Eric to shake, and he does.

"Pleasure."

"Good to meet you," the brown-haired boy says. "My name's Chris. The guy you just shook hands with is Seth's adopted brother Eric, and these two love birds to my left are Seth and Bridgette, respectively."

Toby nods at Seth and Bridgette.

"You new around here, Toby?" Seth asks. Toby notices that Seth is chewing gum with his mouth open. "I haven't seen you around school or anything."

"Um, yeah," Toby says, taking a sip of water. "My parents and I just moved in no more than an hour or two ago."

"You don't say?"

Bridgette leans in. "Wait, your name is Toby?"

Toby nods.

"Toby Lewis-Green? The son of that Lonely Souls group?"

Toby looks surprised. "Uh, yeah. How did you know?"

"It's all this place has talked about since February," Chris says. "You and your parents got into some trouble or something back home, right?"

"No, those are just rumors," Toby says. "My parents wanted to move here to help give back to lesser communities."

"Lesser communities?" Bridgette asks. "What makes Rivers 'lesser'? It doesn't set itself on fire when it gets hot?"

"I don't know, that's just what my parents say."

"Well, what do your parents plan on doing to fix this lesser shit stain of America then, Toby?"

Toby raises his hands in defense, the water bottle in his left. "Look, chick, I don't know. I just got here, and I don't know." He puts his hands down.

"You kids with rich parents like that don't know anything," Seth says.

"I know that you guys are being really rude to a stranger."

"You're not a stranger," Eric says. "You confirmed your name, and your parent's history is on the internet."

"Okay, shut up. Whatever." Toby stands up and takes a sip of water. "What are you guys doing sitting in front of a gas station, anyway?"

Seth takes his arm from around Bridgette, leans back with both hands behind him on the ground, and looks up at Toby. "Just looking for something fun to do, rich boy." He stops chewing and grins. "Got anything *fun* to do?"

"You tell me."

"You like music don't you," Chris says, leaning forward with his arms on his knees. "There's a record store here in Rivers."

"I don't really listen to records," Toby says.

"Well, that's a shame," Bridgette says. "Considering what

your parents do. I mean, did, I guess."

"That's kind of why I don't listen to records. My parents are asses and will just make it all about them if I brought home an album they liked."

Seth's eyes light up. "You know what you should do, rich kid? You should burn down the record store."

All the teens look at Seth with no idea of what he means. "Think about it," he says. "Your parents move here to help better our shitty community, or whatever, right? The two of them are acclaimed musicians trying to avoid bad press, and what do you know? Their son burns down the *local* record store on their first day here."

"It'll be better if you could somehow buy the store, then burn it down," Eric says.

Toby is silent. After all these years, he never could manage to think of a way to get back at his parents for being so selfish, so into themselves, as his mother said. If his parents won't tell him what the fuss is about, Toby could force the truth out of them with more publicity. Plus, he didn't think he would make friends so quickly, and it will probably be a great power move to burn a store down within minutes of meeting them.

"There's a way I could do that," Toby says finally. "My parents have a safe where they keep some cash. I know the combination, so I could go home, look for the safe, and take out some cash. Then I could go to the record store and tell the owner that my parents are interested in buying the place, then we can burn it down."

"You're joking," Eric says.

"No, seriously," Toby says. "Do you guys want to go do this? I can buy matches and stuff here before we go."

Seth grins. "Absolutely."

The four teens get up and accompany Toby inside the

gas station to get matches after Bridgette lets out a: "This is stupid." The group then makes the long walk in the heat to Toby's new house, where Nowell and Brianne have finished moving things in and have left. Upon walking in, Toby runs up the stairs, leaving the other four behind as they look around the mansion in awe. On the top floor, Toby turns left to what he believes is his parents' room. Correct with his guess, he opens the nearest closet, and sitting there on the floor is the safe. Toby gets on his knees, opens the safe, and begins to take out rolls of money, then stops. He realizes he can't walk around carrying rolls of cash in his hands and pockets, so he calls out to the group downstairs. Eric is already in the doorway, and Toby stops mid-yell, startled.

"Oh, um," Eric says, pointing his thumb behind him, "we were just checking out the house."

"That's cool," Toby says. "Hey, um, can one of you guys go to my room, wherever it is, and look for a brown duffle bag for me?"

"Yeah, man," Eric says. He starts to turn around but stops himself. "Hey, I saw some baseball bats in your room. Instead of burning down the store, could we just, like, break some stuff?"

"Yeah, that's fine," Toby says and waves his hand. "Now, go, hurry up before my parents get back."

"Right," Eric says and runs out of the bedroom.

Not long after, Bridgette comes into Nowell and Brianne's room with the duffle bag in her right hand and a baseball bat in the other. She hands Toby the bag.

"Thanks," Toby says.

"No probs," Bridgette says. "Thanks for not being a psycho." She leans down and whispers, "Arson is a serious offense, rich kid." She winks and walks out of the room.

With the money in the bag and each teenager equipped

with a baseball bat, Toby and his newfound friends walk in the heat yet again to the back of the local record store.

"Wait here," Toby says. "I'm gonna go inside and talk to the owner about a deal. Once he leaves, we can smash this place up."

Eric raises his hand and Toby nods to him. "We might want to wait an hour or so. That way no one gets suspicious."

"Okay, fine," Toby says. "See you guys in a bit." He walks through the front door and spots the owner standing behind a counter. Toby approaches the owner, who looks curiously at the duffle bag. Toby puts the duffle bag on the table and says, "Hello, sir. Do you happen to know who I am?"

The owner eyes Toby. "No," he says. "Do you happen to be trading in some CDs?"

"No, sir. I'm the son of Nowell Lewis and Brianne Green, of Lonely Souls. We moved here today."

"I've heard," the owner says. "Now can you please tell me what's in the bag you got here?"

Toby unzips the duffle bag, and the owner's eyes widen upon seeing the money inside. "My parents heard about your store and are interested in making an investment. They're not the biggest fans of writing checks or publicity, so they sent me here to bring you this cash instead."

The owner takes a step back, still looking at the money. He looks at Toby. "Are you fucking joking?"

Toby shakes his head. "No, sir. There's about $250,000 in this bag, just for you."

The owner shakes his head. "No, no, no. First of all, that is not enough money to buy this store. Second of all, I'm not taking any money from some random kid. And finally, I'm calling the fucking police. I don't know what you're up to, but I don't want anything to do with it."

The owner walks to the back of the store to call the police. Panicking, Toby zips up the duffle bag and runs outside to the back of the store.

"How'd it go, rich kid?" Seth asks as he tries to twirl a baseball bat.

"The guy went in the back to call the cops!" Toby screams. "Let's go in there, smash some shit, and head out." He points to Eric. "You stand out front and yell if anyone walks by."

"Aye, aye, captain," Eric says, then does a salute.

The rest of the group immediately runs into the record store and have at it with the baseball bats. CDSs, records, and books are smashed and damaged beyond belief. Chris even manages to knock over a glass case with rare books inside. The owner of the store comes running from the back.

"The cops will be here any minute, you little shits!"

Eric comes through the front door and yells, "Oh shit! Guys, there are some people wondering what's going on. We should probably get out of here!"

The gang runs out of the store and eventually make it back to Toby's house. His parents still gone, Toby puts the money back in the safe while the others put the bats back in his room. They all take a breather in the kitchen.

"That was so scary," Toby says. "We could've gone to juvie or something!"

"*You* still can," Seth says, with a menacing smile.

Toby looks at him, confused. "What do you mean?"

"Why exactly did the guy call the cops?"

"I told him I was my parents' son, and he didn't trust me with the money."

Seth laughs. "You're such a dumbass."

2

NICOTINE SMILE

Nowell and Brianne had read online that Rivers had a growing crime problem, particularly in the realms of drugs and violence. A quick search online does not easily show this fact, however. Upon delving deeper, they learned that the mayor of Rivers has been hiding such acts of crime away from local news outlets. The theory, from the local college paper, among others, is that the mayor wants to maintain a safe and friendly atmosphere for the college town. Any and all news relating to stabbings, robberies, drug busts, and personal items missing from cars damages the reputation of the small city.

Naturally, once Nowell and Brianne decided that Rivers was the small city they wanted to relocate to, bringing down crime was at the top of their list. One week after moving to Rivers and settling down, Nowell and Brianne met with the mayor of Rivers, Mayor Waterston, to discuss action that needed to be done to aid the betterment of the community. The discussion proved fruitful, as Mayor Waterston quickly decided that there must be a press conference in front of the

Rivers Police Department downtown so the couple could announce their intentions for the community to the media.

During this press conference, which is being filmed live for all the country to see, Nowell and Brianne announce that they are very grateful to be accepted into the humble, small city. The couple also express that they feel that work needs to be done for those that are free and for those that are behind bars. Their solution is that those that are behind bars must now do mandatory community service, no matter the crime. Nowell states that everyone in the country deserves a second chance, but others must be willing to lend a helping hand. Brianne states that after having a great talk with the intelligent Mayor Waterston, proper rehabilitation "can" be achieved as long as all the residents of the small city pitch in.

"What do you mean by 'can' be achieved, Brianne?" a local reporter asks.

"Well," Brianne says, taking off her designer shades to let the crowd know that she is serious, "when Nowell and I talked to the mayor earlier regarding letting all those imprisoned get a second chance, he was apprehensive."

"Apprehensive how?"

"He informed us," Nowell says, leaning closer to his mic at the podium, "that it would be a risky move to let *all* of those behind bars receive a second chance. And that if we were to take a risk, we as in the Rivers community, then the tax rates must be increased."

The crowd before Nowell, Brianne, and Mayor Waterston do not take kindly to the insidiousness of the mayor raising the tax rates as a repercussion to helping his own people. Many did not believe he held this power. Nevertheless, there is an immediate and tremendous roar amongst the crowd.

When given an opening, Nowell speaks again. "When Brianne and I spoke with the mayor earlier, we told him that he is doing a disservice to his people. By keeping crime out of the news, by not taking this opportunity to properly rehabilitate his fellow citizens, and by simply and unwaveringly following the path of greed by choosing to take money from your pockets."

Brianne adds into her microphone, "We accepted the mayor's offer to have this press conference to show him what his people really want with his own eyes." She looks to her left toward Mayor Waterston. "What is your decision, Mayor Waterston?"

Mayor Waterston, clearly aghast from the turn of events, red in the face, turns away from Brianne and walks off the stage. He can clearly be seen entering the back of a limo to be escorted out.

"You see, people of Rivers," Nowell says, raising his left arm toward the limo while facing the crowd. "Your mayor has walked away instead of helping us grow as a community." He places both hands on the podium on stage. "It is up to all of us to make a change to this city, to make it a better place for all of us and the generations to come." He stands in front of the podium and Brianne follows suit. "Who's with me?" he screams. The crowd roars, and many begin to advance toward the stage to join Nowell and Brianne.

Meanwhile, Toby is watching the press conference unfold on television at Seth and Eric's house. The three teenagers, plus Chris and Bridgette, are sitting at a round kitchen table, eyes glued to the television.

"Look at this," Seth says, spitting gum into a nearby trash can. "I guess I gotta hand it to them to wait a week to pull some kind of publicity stunt." He looks to his right at Toby. "How much did your folks pay off Mayor Waterston to pretend he wouldn't give everyone a get out of jail free card?"

"Yeah," Chris says, putting down a soda can, "Mayor Waterston loves Rivers."

"I don't think it's a stunt, you guys," Toby says. He had been spending most of his days in Rivers with his new friends, although he used the term loosely regarding Seth and Bridgette. Toby found that Chris and Eric seem to enjoy his company, and Eric had invited him over to his house every day, so far. However, not long after Toby shows up to spend time with the two brothers, Bridgette always shows up, presumably to spend time with Seth. Toby believes that Seth is too hostile toward him and his parents, while Bridgette comes off as confrontational only toward him. "My parents haven't done any actual work since I've been born, so I don't think they have much political sway, local or not."

"I'm telling you," Seth says, "they bought him off."

"It does seem a little iffy, Toby," Bridgette says, turning down the volume with a remote. "Maybe you don't know your parents that well--just like everyone else."

"Okay," Toby says. He stands from his wooden chair, grabs the remote from Bridgette's hand, and turns off the television. Bridgette has an offended look on her face as Toby continues, "Why don't we go downtown and see?"

"How does that solve anything?" Eric asks, looking over at his friends.

"I don't know," Toby says. "Maybe if we all go, we can feel if the vibe is wrong or something."

"It feels sketchy from here," Bridgette says, arms crossed and leaning back in her chair.

"Well, we can't go off what the TV is showing us," Toby says, briefly pointing the remote at the television. "Let's go see in person."

The other four friends think it over and ultimately decide that they should go downtown. After braving the heat, the five teenagers make it to the Rivers Police Department where the press conference turned rally has grown larger. Some of the citizens of Rivers have brought the materials to create signs protesting Mayor Waterston and his mistreatment of the inmates and prisoners of the small city. One of the participants approaches Toby.

"Hey," the man says, "are you Nowell and Brianne's son?"

Toby replies yes, and the man hands Toby a sign and states how much he loves the music of Lonely Souls and the message of the songs that still persists to this day. Toby thanks the man, and the man goes on his way.

"This is pretty cool," Eric says a few minutes later. "Getting involved with our community."

"Stunt," Seth says, looking around. He spots something and squints. "Hey, Chris, is that your uncle?"

Seth points, and the group of friends looks. In the distance, Chris's uncle, a man with long and scraggly brown hair with a leather jacket, is sitting on top of a sports car, cross-legged. Sitting beside him is a woman wearing a jean jacket, and the two share a cigarette. When the woman takes a puff, their uncle leans over to the woman's ear, hand hiding his mouth as if he wants no one to see what he's saying, and after a few seconds, the woman laughs. Then the two share a passionate kiss.

"That's my uncle," Chris says, "but that sure as hell isn't my aunt."

Before anyone can respond, Chris walks through the crowd, friends following close behind, to confront his uncle. Before reaching him, the uncle spots the teenagers, puts out the cigarette, and gets up to stand in front of the car.

"Chrissy," the uncle says with a nicotine smile. "Here to support our fellow inmates?"

"Who the hell is that woman, and what were you doing kissing her just a moment ago?"

The uncle feigns a confused face. "You mean you're not here to be an active member of this community? For shame, Chrissy." He ruffles Chris's hair, but Chris smacks his uncle's right hand away from him.

"Don't call me Chrissy, and don't bullshit me, Richard."

Richard punches Chris in the stomach, who then falls to the ground. Richard then grabs Chris by the hair to make Chris look up at him as the other four teenagers take a step back.

"Don't talk to adults, especially your fucking family, like that, you little shit." He pushes Chris to the ground onto his back. Eric and Bridgette go to Chris and squat down to check on him.

Richard looks at Toby. "You," he says, pointing. "Don't go running home telling your mommy and daddy what you just saw."

"I won't," Toby says.

Richard walks to the driver's door of the sports car, opens it, and takes out a brown paper bag. He closes the door, steps over Chris on the ground, and walks to Toby. "Here," Richard says. He hands over the bag to Toby, and Toby takes it. "Share it amongst yourselves. You are all gonna need them." He then turns around and whistles to the woman. "Let's go!" The two get in the sports car, reverse to turn around, and then speed away.

Toby and Seth join the others on the ground, and Chris leans the top half of his body up.

"Are you okay, man?" Toby asks.

"Yeah," Chris says, lightly coughing. He nods toward the bag in Toby's hand. "What's in there?"

The others look at Toby, who lays the dingy bag on the ground and opens it. Inside the bag are a .22 caliber hand-gun, a 20-round box of ammo, and six nickel bags of cocaine.

3

BLUE MOON

Six days after the rambunctious rally in front of the Rivers Police Department, Mayor Waterston fulfilled Nowell and Brianne's wish to provide mandatory community service to inmates and prisoners. The announcement was filmed at Mayor Waterston's home in his study, with Nowell and Brianne standing on either side of him as Mayor Waterston sat in his accent chair. Talks regarding the issue post-press conference were kept behind doors, so there were no protesters outside of Mayor Waterston's home and only a handful of camera crew workers.

The small city of Rivers rejoiced upon hearing the news and many of the civilians congregated in front of the Rivers Police Department to celebrate. After leaving the home of Mayor Waterston, Nowell and Brianne joined the crowd before walking on the stage, which had been left there since the press conference.

Nowell announced that today was a great victory for the Rivers community, but he and Brianne would not stop there. Brianne stated that starting tomorrow, there would be a rally outside the Rivers Detention Center to bring word of this achievement across the country. The crowd cheered, and Nowell and Brianne held each other's hand in the air to symbolize unity, an action that made the crowd cheer louder.

That night, Nowell and Brianne go home, bringing with them Chinese food to eat for dinner. To bring Toby his meal, Brianne goes up the stairs and to the right to knock on Toby's door. Before Toby can get out a 'Just a minute', Brianne opens his bedroom door, announcing that she has dinner.

"Mom, wait, no," Toby exclaims.

In his room, Brianne sees Toby in front of his bed, trying to hide the .22 and three of the nickel bags lying out on his bed with his body, the brown paper bag a few inches away. Toby isn't quick enough, and Brianne screams, "Oh my God!" before dropping Toby's Chinese food on his bedroom floor.

"Nowell!" Brianne yells. "Get up here, now!"

Nowell runs up the stairs, asking what's going on, and makes it to Toby's open bedroom door to his wife's side. At first, he sees the Chinese food on the floor, but then sees the horror his wife is witnessing.

"What is going on here?" Nowell screams.

Toby grabs the nickel bags and the .22--the latter causing Brianne to scream and hide her face in Nowell's chest--and puts them in the dingy brown paper bag.

"Mom, Dad, I can explain," Toby says, with his hands in front of him.

"Who gave you that stuff, Son?" Nowell asks, rubbing Brianne's back with his left hand while her face is still in his chest.

"I honestly don't know if it's safe to tell you," Toby says, "but I haven't done anything wrong, I promise."

"If you haven't done anything wrong, then why can't you tell us?"

Toby takes a step closer, his hands slightly lowered. "Dad, I don't want you guys causing any more trouble here in Rivers."

"Any more trouble?" Nowell asks. He moves Brianne's face from his chest and looks at her. "Did you hear that, Bri?"

Brianne, face red and moist with tears, says, "Yes, I did." She steps back away from Nowell and turns to Toby. "Your father and I just made community service mandatory for the inmates and prisoners of this humble city, and you have the nerve to tell *us* we're causing trouble?"

"Mom, I--" Toby begins but is then cut off.

"No," Brianne says with a swipe of her right hand. She walks toward Toby and pushes him to the side, causing him to bump his behind on an end table.

"Hey!" Toby exclaims.

Brianne grabs the brown bag from Toby's bed and walks back to Nowell, who has his arms crossed at the bedroom door.

"If you can't tell us who gave this to you," Brianne says, with her arm extended out to point the bag toward Toby, "then you can't leave this house until further notice."

"Mom, that's bullshit! I didn't do anything!"

Nowell walks past Brianne, who is now holding the brown bag at her side, and he slaps Toby across the face before pointing his finger at him.

"You watch your language, especially when you talk to your mother and me. As she said, you're grounded until further notice."

Nowell turns away from his son and goes to exit the

bedroom before accidentally stepping in the Chinese food on the floor. He looks down at it, then to Toby. "Again, dinner is ready." He and Brianne leave the bedroom and close the door.

As promised, the next day, exactly one week after Nowell and Brianne's initial proposal, members of the Rivers community met outside the Rivers Detention Center with the couple. The rally garnered an even greater crowd than the week before, and the media presence was more notable. All the excitement was not enjoyed by Toby, of course, as he was ordered to remain at home. That evening, however, while Nowell and Brianne are still out fighting their cause, Toby hears a smack on his window. Toby, who is lying in bed, gets up and walks over to the window. After letting up the window shade, he is greeted by Bridgette smiling at him, so he opens the window up.

"Hi, there," Bridgette says, bringing her right leg through the window, then herself.

Toby steps back to let her in. "Uh, hi. What are you doing here?"

Bridgette stands in the middle of the room, observing it. "Well," she says, brushing dirt off her jean shorts, "I was watching the news at Seth and Eric's place and saw your parents on the TV."

"Yeah," Toby says. "They're having their stupid victory rally." He goes over to this bed to sit down, but Bridgette stops him, grabbing him by the arm.

Seeing the confusion on Toby's face, Bridgette says, "So I came here to check on you." She lets go of his arm. "Did you know there's a blue moon out, right now?"

"What's a blue moon?"

"It's like an extra full moon, but sometimes it can be blue."

Toby nods toward the window. "Is it blue out there right now?"

Bridgette smiles and walks back to the window. "There's only one way to find out." She then turns around and climbs back out the window, onto the roof. Toby follows her out the window to see her sitting down on the roof, looking at the moon. He sits beside her.

"Isn't it beautiful," Bridgette says.

"It does look nice," Toby says. He looks at Bridgette. "Thank you for coming to check on me."

Bridgette gives Toby a quick glance. "No prob, dude. I don't know how you haven't gone crazy living with your psycho parents."

Toby, looking back at the moon, says, "They mean well. But, seriously, thank you. I don't have my phone, but I have a good feeling you didn't bother calling." He sighs and curls his legs up toward his chest, arms around his legs. Bridgette gives him a faintly concerned look.

"You alright?" she asks.

"I just wish that they would stay out of the spotlight sometimes, you know? Like, back when I was a little kid—when it was simpler."

"Well," Bridgette says, "they were out of the news for a while there. They just came back strong."

Toby looks down at his shoes and sighs. "Yeah, I guess you're right. I'm just worried about them, and me, I guess, that's all. You know they found that bag that Chris's uncle gave me."

Bridgette's eyes light up. "Holy shit. What did they do?"

Toby chuckles. "They grounded me and took my phone. My mom took the bag somewhere. That's why I'm here while they're off achieving moral victories—or whatever they call it." He stretches out his legs and leans back on his arms. "You know, I don't even think they were all that concerned about the gun, just the coke."

"Why do you say that?" Bridgette asks, focusing on Toby's face.

"Well, you know the stigma about rich kids. They were probably afraid I was going to become another statistic." Toby pauses. "I'm sometimes afraid of that, too. It's like, I don't ever have to work in my life if I don't want to. I peaked the moment I was born."

Bridgette turns to face her body toward Toby. "That can't be all bad."

"I can end up like my parents."

Bridgette looks down at the panelling of the roof. "Yeah."

Toby gets on his knees, looking at the moon. "I know they're good people. I mean, all people have some good in their hearts. Even my parents, as self-centered as they can be, quit the music industry to raise me. Only me." Toby looks at Bridgette, and they make eye contact. "By the end of this—my life, that is—I just hope it's not only me."

"I feel that, " Bridgette says. "I also crave that"—she glances at the moon—"consistency you had when you were a kid." She looks back at him, fidgeting with her hands. "I, uh..." She laughs to herself and looks down. "This is silly, but I've been doing these commercials. For like cereal and yogurt and stuff." She then looks back at Toby. "You know, to make a little money, at first. But, eventually, I'd like to get out of Rivers. This is a city where you can get trapped forever, and I don't want that to happen to me."

"That's not really silly," Toby says. "I mean, you have a portfolio, and who knows, someone might see you in a commercial and cast you for an episode in a show or something."

Bridgette smiles and turns her head to look at the moon.

"Yeah, maybe someday. I just...don't want to end up like my mom." She looks back at Toby. "She, uh, she killed herself when I was a baby. Some kind of drug overdose my dad says."

"I'm sorry you had to go through that," Toby says, extending his right arm to rub Bridgette's knee.

Bridgette begins to tear up. "Thanks. I mean"—she looks back at Toby—"I never really *knew* her, you know? It just would've been cool to have a mom to be pissed off at sometimes." Toby stops rubbing her knee and Bridgette laughs. "I'm also afraid of drowning." She rubs her left eye. "I can't swim, so drowning would suck."

Toby chuckles. "Yeah, that would suck."

Bridgette looks back at the moon, silent except for sniffling, then she turns back to Toby and says, "I don't know if I'm too pessimistic, I mean, I'm not *trying* to be, but I don't think it's about everyone being good in their hearts."

Toby looks at her for a few silent moments, then asks, "What do you think it's about?"

"I think," she sniffles, then says, "that we're all kinda doomed to our fate. Like, we can try and try, but we can't really change who we are because it's all predetermined. I don't think my mom ever had a chance, and I'm okay with that."

"As long as we *try* to do good then that's all that matters," Toby says.

Bridgette looks back at him, sympathy in her eyes. "Yeah." She stands up and stretches. "I should probably go home and eat dinner."

"Oh, yeah," Toby says, standing up. "Um, thank you again for coming to see me, Bridgette."

Bridgette puts her hands in her jacket pockets and nods.

"Anytime, Toby." She begins to walk toward the edge of the roof.

"Oh," Toby says, pointing his thumb toward his bedroom window, "you can go out the door."

"Nah, I'll just shimmy down this pillar just like I came up."

"Okay."

Bridgette crouches down at the edge of the roof, and Toby begins to crawl through his window. Before he gets inside, Bridgette says, "Toby?"

Toby looks at Bridgette, his body halfway into his room. "Yeah?"

"I feel less alone knowing you understand."

4

———

I'M FINDING IT HARDER TO BE A GENTLEMAN

The next morning while eating breakfast with his parents, Toby asked Nowell and Brianne if his grounding could end. He confessed to his parents that a man at the rally the previous week gave him the bag and simply drove off, though Toby did not specify who the man was. Toby claims that he kept the bag in his room to make sure the contents did not get into the wrong hands since simply discarding the bag could lead to just that. He also admitted that he had no real plan on what to do with the bag once he brought it home.

Nowell and Brianne look at each other from across the kitchen table for a few moments, then decide that Toby is right. Brianne apologizes to Toby for not letting him defend himself, and Nowell apologizes "for any harm done." Upon finishing breakfast, Nowell heads upstairs and comes back down with Toby's cellphone. Toby thanks his parents, who tell him they love him, and proceeds to walk outside and sit on the porch step. Toby turns his phone on, ignores his missed messages, and searches 'things to do in Rivers.' After a couple minutes of scrolling, Toby decides that he should visit the Rivers Petting Zoo and immediately calls Bridgette.

The previous night meant a lot to Toby as he felt that he had his first genuine conversation with anyone in his whole life, and he does not want to let that go. By calling Bridgette, and maybe taking her on an unofficial secret date, Toby hopes to maybe continue their heart-to-heart to strengthen the new relationship. Toby knows that Bridgette is in a relationship with Seth, but maybe more one-on-one time could prove to Bridgette that Toby is a more suitable candidate.

"Hello," Bridgette says.

Toby stands up quickly. "Hey, Bridgette," he says a little too excitedly. He walks off the front steps and begins to pace, rubbing the back of his head occasionally.

"Oh, hey, Toby," Bridgette says. "How did you get your phone? I thought you were grounded."

"Oh, yeah, I was. I literally just convinced my parents to free me a few minutes ago."

"Oh, cool!"

"So, uh," Toby says, then clears his throat, "what are you up to today? I figured we could hang out or something since I'm available again."

"I'm just at home memorizing lines for a yogurt commercial."

"Yeah, how's that going?"

"Awful. I could really get out of the house. I don't care if it's hot."

"Perfect," Toby says. "Well, um, I saw online that Rivers has a petting zoo. Do you want to go? No one should be there since all the college kids are out of town."

"Yeah! I'll meet you there in an hour."

Bridgette hangs up the phone, and Toby does a double-take to make sure he didn't lose connection.

"One hour," he says to himself. "Awesome."

Toby and Bridgette meet at the front of the Rivers Petting Zoo & Play Place and greet each other. "So rich kid likes animals, huh?" Bridgette asks him as they walk through the front gates.

"Yeah," Toby says with his hands in his pockets. "When I was four, my dad had gotten us this short-haired dachshund that was *super* independent—so independent that he ran away a few weeks after we got him."

"Oh, my god," Bridgette says, putting her hands up to her mouth. "Were you okay?"

"Yeah. Sometimes people leave, and dogs aren't any different."

"I guess so," Bridgette says, putting her hands in her jacket pockets. "I, uh, never had any pets growing up. My dad would ask *me* if I wanted a dog or something like that, but I always told him no. I'm afraid of them running away." She waves her finger at Toby. "I almost got a bearded dragon, though. They don't feel the need to leave you behind."

"If you don't mind me asking," Toby says, "how is your dad? You know, raising you all by himself."

"I think he's done a great job, considering the circumstances. I, uh, trust him. More than anything in the world." She and Toby stop by an area with several lambs and start to pet and feed them. "My dad has always been so patient with me, and I *love* it when people can give off this sense of calm. Just being around someone like that works wonders. No matter who they are, that patience makes you feel loved. He also manages a comedy club here in Rivers. He's super funny, so sometimes when I'm feeling down, he'll crack a joke that'll crack me up. He says he told a lot of them to my mom when she was alive."

"Do you think he misses your mom still?"

"I don't know," Bridgette says, crouching down by a lamb. "I miss her. I don't remember her, like, at all. But I miss her." She reaches down her jacket and takes out a watch locket. She stands up and opens the locket to show Toby. Inside is a picture of a woman holding a baby, both of them smiling. "I wear this around my neck every day, and I look at it whenever I'm down." She closes it. "I know that people are who they are, and my mom couldn't really change her outcome, but she was at least happy at some point in her life. And looking at that picture of us gives me hope that I could always be happy." The two of them move away from the area with the lambs and explore more of the petting zoo.

"What else makes you happy?" Toby asks.

"I really like acting. I mean, right now it's just commercials. But Rivers High has school plays that I hope to be in next year. I really feel alive when I'm being someone else."

"Even in a commercial?"

"Yeah," Bridgette says, pulling her hair into a ponytail. "Just being able to see through the eyes of someone else helps you understand their experience. It doesn't matter if it's them tasting their favorite bowl of cereal or finding out they have cancer. It's life. Plus, acting requires hard work and a lot of cooperation if you're on set."

The two of them make it to the back of the petting zoo where the ponies and zebras are.

"Do you think being an actor is the most consistent lifestyle there is?" Toby asks, feeding a pony.

"I think it can be as consistent as I want it to be," Bridgette says, then looks at Toby. "I mean, you and your parents are famous, and you guys seem to be doing fine." She looks back at a zebra and feeds it.

"Well, they're musicians," Toby says. "Soul ones, at that. They draw a lot of attention to themselves, but they're not rock stars."

Bridgette laughs. "No, they definitely aren't."

Toby stops feeding the animals and looks at Bridgette. "What's that supposed to mean?"

Bridgette looks up, sees the expression on Toby's face, and shakes her head. "Oh, I didn't mean any offense! I just mean that I don't care for their music, that's all."

"You don't like Lonely Souls?"

"It's...kinda boring to me," Bridgette says sheepishly. "I think soul music should focus more on the vibe, the energy, the actual music. But I think your mom and dad tend to focus on lyrics."

"Well, what kind of artists do you listen to?"

"I like Pregnancy Brain and People Person on Paper."

"Pregnancy Brain!" Toby exclaims. "That's soft rock! I get PPP because that's more alternative, but you think Pregnancy Brain has more exciting music than my parents?"

"Not more exciting, just more *about* the music compared to your parents. There's a sense of harmony I feel with Pregnancy Brain."

"Fair enough," Toby says, raising his hands and smiling.

Toby and Bridgette walk around the petting zoo some more and then spot a pigpen. Bridgette gets really excited upon seeing the pigs, jumping up and down before telling Toby the two must pet the pigs. Upon Toby saying yes, Bridgette runs over to the pigpen and squats down to pet them. Toby slowly catches up with Bridgette and squats down beside her.

"Don't you think it's sad," Toby says while petting a pig, "that this is probably the best thing in their life?"

"The little piggies?"

"All of the animals, really. I mean, these guys get to walk around in mud and play in their own shit. But those other guys, like the zebras, can't really roam around in their own habitat."

"I think it's good for them," Bridgette says, adjusting a wristband on her arm after a pig tries to eat it. "I think this is a better alternative than being hunted by lions every day. Or getting cooked up into bacon like these guys." She grabs a pig's face and shakes it playfully, talking baby talk to it. "There are two ways to be free," she says after.

"I don't think they're free. They literally have this wood here to keep them in. Maybe if they were born here this is their idea of freedom. But coming here from the wild, like the zebras, must be the worst thing in their life."

"They're animals, Toby," Bridgette says. "They're smarter than we think, but I don't think they have the capacity to think 'this is the worst.' They have harmony here, not the stupid despair of knowing they're fucked from the jump... like people."

"It doesn't change the fact that they're not free."

Bridgette looks at Toby. "It makes all the difference. The worst things these animals have to deal with is that they get taken care of and different people every day get to pet and feed them. Take me, for example, some nobody from Rivers, USA. My mother had depression, a drug addiction, and she *killed herself* after having me. Not only that, but *I*, her only daughter who will probably inherit these problems, found her freaking heroin kit while cleaning the basement one day."

"You found what?"

"That's not important," Bridgette says, shaking her head. She stands up. "What I mean is, these animals here have a good life. They don't ever have to worry about anyone leaving them forever or failure or disappointment." She looks down at the pigs. "They can just be pigs." She looks back at Toby. "Surely, you must envy that."

Toby stands up. "What do you mean?"

"You were forced into a life with no privacy, with rich parents and the world watching their every move. Sooner or later, the world will be watching you."

"You said last night that my parents have been out of the public eye for a while."

"Yeah, I did," Bridgette says. "But people don't change, Toby. And you're seeing that now with the stupid antics your parents have been up to. If you're a pig, you don't have to worry about your rich psycho parents moving across the country and potentially destroying your whole life. As a human boy who craves the consistency of the life of a pig, *you* do, Toby."

Toby closes his eyes and does a quick stomp on the ground. "Don't call my parents psychos. They're good people, and I think you should apologize for what you said."

"I didn't say anything worth apologizing for, and don't you stomp the ground at me."

"Well, you're kind of being rude, and it's frustrating."

"I'm just having a conversation, Toby," Bridgette says, crossing her arms. "It's not my fault you can't handle a difference of opinion."

"Whatever," Toby says. He walks past Bridgette, intentionally bumping into her.

"Hey, watch it, asshole," Bridgette says, then kicks Toby in the back of his left leg.

"Ow!" Toby screams. He grabs his leg for a moment, then turns around. He attempts to push Bridgette, but Bridgette grabs both of his arms.

"Don't you fucking touch me, you freak," Bridgette says as she and Toby fall into the pigpen.

5

———

THE INDIE DARLINGS OF PALEVIEW

In 1995, Nowell gets off a plane in The States after visiting the United Kingdom. It's the dead of winter, and he is freezing in his trench coat that he bought abroad. In the parking lot outside of the airport, he finds his car, drops his keys as he takes them out of his pocket, and unlocks the door. He puts his singular suitcase in the trunk and then gets in the driver's seat, sitting there for fifteen minutes as the car heats up. He sighs, then proceeds to drive out of the parking lot, onto the interstate. After driving for about thirty-five miles, he makes it to his hometown of Paleview. Instead of driving straight to his house, he stops and parks in front of the local soul and jazz club, The Neo Lounge. He gets out of the car and proceeds to walk in, being greeted by the warm air, lively music, and red lights.

The Neo Lounge has few visitors tonight due to the freezing weather, which Nowell doesn't mind. He takes a seat right in the back of the main area and watches the performance that is center stage. It is a raven-haired woman, crooning the words:

Wanton frolics through fields of May

Patched out bullets and thoughts of brains
Visit the rosy hotel of our room
Boss man, or woman, up to you
We are stars with the heartstrings of guitars who
Always manage to feel fine in
A whore-filled wasteland filled with
Lonely Souls who try to drag us down, a unit who just
Always wear our Sunday best while there's something
burning
We'll sing of California and scoff at the fumes of cigarettes
Oh, I'll fly anywhere with you if you keep me begging for
another kiss

The woman says a calm, "Thank you" upon completing her song, and the few attendees of the Neo Lounge clap for her. She promptly walks off stage and out through the front hall that Nowell came in.

Nowell gets out of his seat and follows her down the hall. By this time, the woman is standing outside the Neo Lounge, leaning against the brick wall. She lights a cigarette as Nowell walks out.

"What about scoffing at those things," he says, smiling.

"It's just a song, sweetie," she says. She's wearing a brown fur coat now with her red dress.

Nowell grabs the cigarette from her hand and tosses it on the ground, crushing it with his right shoe. "There are other addictions that can help you stay warm, dear," he says.

The woman looks at him, mouth ajar, but in a more amused way. "Oh," she says, crossing her arms, mostly from the cold. "Give me an example, then."

Nowell leans in closer to her, leaning his right side on the brick wall. "Where did you learn to sing like that?"

"Self-trained. Why do you ask?"

"I know a guy in England. Well, he's not from England,

he's just there, right now, on business. He's a music producer, and he produces indie acts like yourself."

"You know a guy from England? And how do you know him?"

"Oh, I've known him since I was twelve. I just flew back from England after supporting him."

"How old are you now, stranger?" the woman asks.

"Oh, I'm sorry," Nowell says, using his left hand to take a glove off the other. He extends his hand to the woman, smiling again. "My name's Nowell Lewis, and I'm twenty years old."

The woman shakes Nowell's hand. "Looks like we have something in common. My name is Brianne Green. Two Ns."

Nowell puts his glove back on. "Pleasure to meet you, Two Ns. Mind if I call you Bri?"

"I don't see why not," Brianne says with the faintest grin.

"Great," Nowell says. He slightly turns toward the door to the Neo Lounge. "Now, Bri, do you mind if we go back inside? I crushed your only source of warmth."

Brianne nods quickly with a "Yes, yes," and the two go back inside. "Do you have the kind of money to fly back and forth to England?"

"Oh, no," Nowell says as they make their way to the main area. "Elisha takes care of my plane tickets. This is America, Brianne. No one has any money. No one who's honest, at least."

Nowell sits in the seat he was in earlier, and Brianne sits in the one beside him.

"Is your indie producer friend Elisha honest?"

Nowell takes off his coat, revealing a plain white T with red sleeve ends. He lays the coat on the table in front of them. "As honest as a man could ever be. You know, he'll be flying back here to the states himself in a couple of days. You can meet him in person."

"Maybe I will."

"You definitely will," Nowell says, turning his whole body to the right to face Brianne, his legs dangling over the arm of the chair.

Brianne laughs. "And what makes you so sure?"

"Because I am going to change your life forever."

"Oh, yeah?"

"Yes, Bri." Nowell gets out of the chair and turns it to face Brianne. He then grabs the seat she's in and turns it to face him. He sits down and cups her hands in his. "You have an incredible voice, and I don't want you to be another lonely soul in this world, in this country, who will be lost or forgotten to time."

"You can't fight time, Nowell."

"Maybe not, but we can leave our mark." Nowell scoots his chair a few inches closer to Brianne and brings her hand closer to him. "Do you want to leave your mark on the world?"

Brianne did want to leave her mark on the world. After brief consideration, Brianne nods and decides to take Nowell's offer to meet Elisha in two days. Nowell and Brianne exchange numbers, and Nowell informs her that he will call her the moment Elisha arrives.

The next day, Brianne receives a phone call from Nowell. She answers it with excitement, and Nowell tells her to meet him at the local record store, Manny's Records, in twenty-five minutes. Brianne quickly gets dressed and runs to the record store. Walking inside, she spots Nowell in the rock section.

"Glad you can make it," Nowell says, giving Brianne a light smile before going back to skimming the records.

"Where's Elisha?"

"Oh, he doesn't come in until tomorrow."

Brianne playfully smacks Nowell's left arm. "Are you freaking serious? What's so important then?"

Nowell laughs and turns to Brianne. "Okay, first, ow. Second, I want you to come to my place, or we can go to yours, and listen to an album of your choosing."

"You're joking."

"No, I'm not." Nowell begins to walk down the aisle. "What do you listen to?"

Brianne follows him. "Pop."

Nowell scoffs. "Yeah, right." He puts his hands in his pockets. "Stop fucking with me, I'm being serious."

Brianne is walking side by side with Nowell now. Arms crossed, she says, "People Person on Paper."

Nowell stops and looks at Brianne. "Oh, keeping it local, I see! Cool Brianne here likes PPP."

"You don't?"

"I do, trust me. That where you get your soul voice? Eddy is such an incredibly unique singer for the genre."

"No, but they helped."

Nowell nods. "Right on. Well, hey, do you have their album? We can just listen to that and geek out or whatever."

Brianne agrees, so they both exit Manny's Records and get into Nowell's car—who apologizes for not driving Brianne home the night before since he didn't know she did not have a vehicle. They then drive to Brianne's apartment, with her giving him directions. Once there, they walk in, and Brianne apologizes to Nowell for the heater, as it is 'quite spotty.' She tells him to make himself at home after she takes her jacket and boots off and walks into the kitchen.

Nowell sits on a couch in the living room while Brianne

makes tea, and the two talk about musical influences—Nowell leaning more toward punk and the growing soul scene in Paleview. Brianne's taste lies more with what the meaning of the songs are and less so about the sound. Nowell says he could tell based on her song from the night before as he found it beautiful.

Brianne hands Nowell a cup of tea, he thanks her, and then she goes over to the corner of the room to play the People Person on Paper album. The music begins, Brianne sits beside Nowell, and the two sip tea together, telling each other fun facts about the band and the album. Brianne has more to say than Nowell, particularly about the next to last song on side A. She tells Nowell that the story behind the track is that a woman's lover has left her for another and that the lover's feelings for the woman were never true. The woman tries to move on from the relationship, but after many years, she finds out where her ex-lover lives and attempts to kill her. The ex-lover, however, was one step ahead of the woman and shoots the woman in the leg before reaffirming that her love is for another. The ex-lover then shoots the woman in the heart and leaves town with her true love.

Nowell finds the story to be quite morbid, but instead, he tells Brianne that she has beautiful eyes. The two lay their teacups down on the floor and share a passionate kiss, and they continue to do so as the pop from the label of side A repeats.

Nowell stays the night at Brianne's apartment, and the next day he introduces her to Elisha, a handsome dark-skinned man who is impressed by both Brianne's vocal capabilities and her lyrics.

"'Lonely Souls,'" Elisha says. "That's what we should call ourselves."

The three decide they will form a soul music group that focuses more on the lyrics rather than mood and sound, and a four-album contract is made. They write a few songs and record some, but Elisha's frequent trips back and forth to the United Kingdom make making music difficult. In the summer of 1996, with Elisha's blessing, Nowell and Brianne make Lonely Souls a two-person show after Elisha decides to live in England permanently to handle his up-and-coming record label. With Elisha out of the group, Nowell and Brianne are forced to strip down the musical approach to the songs, oftentimes having tracks be only around two minutes long.

That fall, Nowell and Brianne get married. There is no announcement of an engagement beforehand. Nowell wakes up one morning as Brianne is eating pancakes and simply tells her, "I want to marry you." They are made husband and wife later that day.

In the next few months, Nowell and Brianne make significant progress with their songwriting, and Elisha begins the marketing campaign for their debut album: *Ataraxic.*

"I want people to feel free when they hear this album," Brianne says. "Free from worry. To feel a sense of...calm wash over them while the music takes over their senses."

In March of 1997, *Ataraxic* is released worldwide to critical acclaim. Sales are steady, and after two months, the album has sold 500,000 copies. By that summer, Nowell and Brianne are called the indie darlings of Paleview and begin touring across the country. They are already hard at work on their next album by the end of the year, *Ataraxic* making many year-end lists.

For their second album, Nowell and Brianne write more about their relationship and the strength that love carries.

After much anticipation, *Biennial* is released to further critical and commercial success and goes on to be considered one of the best albums of all time. *Biennial* makes the couple superstars, and Lonely Souls begin a world tour; however, the hectic schedule triggers a short-lived drinking problem for Nowell, who sometimes lashes out in interviews regarding the release of the next album from Lonely Souls.

"You want to know why we named our album *Biennial*?" Nowell asks an interviewer. "Because you can't rush this stuff, man. It takes two years, *minimum*, and we can't **** this up. We wanted to make an album where every two years, when you revisit it, you find something new, and it means something different to you. We want all our music to be like that."

Lonely Souls begin work on their third album one month after their world tour ends. Nowell and Brianne need this time to decompress, and Nowell stops drinking, although he does begin to recreationally use marijuana. The break is beneficial to Nowell and Brianne as not only does their relationship grow stronger, but their creative output increases tenfold. For all of 2000, the two are hard at work and announce that they will be making a double album to be released in March 2001, four years after *Ataraxic*.

The untitled third album from Lonely Souls is even more anticipated than *Biennial,* and Nowell and Brianne try their hardest to keep both their personal lives and their recording process under wraps. Then, in December of 2000, one of Nowell and Brianne's maids goes to the media claiming she has a big secret regarding the married couple. It does not take long for a news channel to pick her up for an interview. There has been speculation that Nowell cheated on Brianne with the maid and the maid is now pregnant.

The maid announces that this is not true and that instead, Brianne is pregnant, and she and Nowell are planning on aborting the baby. The story proves controversial, and Elisha calls Nowell and Brianne to let them know that they need to set the record straight or their four-album contract would be broken. In an interview two days later, Nowell and Brianne announce that it is indeed true that Brianne is pregnant with their first child. They state that it is a lie that the couple were aborting the baby, but rather they are retiring from music to take care of it. They announced that their long-anticipated third album, *Moribund,* will be released in two short weeks.

This news takes the media by storm. After the interview, Nowell and Brianne get in their limo to be returned home. Once they are out of the public eye, Brianne covers her face with both hands and starts crying.

$$6$$

I SAT BY THE OCEAN

In the present day, Nowell and Brianne wake up early in the morning with plans of buying a sports yacht. After spending their time in Rivers rallying, the couple decides they've earned a well-deserved break and want to spend some time alone on the water. The two drive out of town to the nearest boat shop and purchase the first sports yacht they see.

"It goes up to a hundred miles an hour," says the shop owner. "I'm not sure what you're planning on doing, but if you need to flee from the cops or anything like that this should do the trick."

"We're just trying to get some alone time," Brianne says, her designer shades matching her raven hair. She writes the shop owner a check and hands it to him.

"Thank you for doing business with us, Ms. Green," the owner says, putting the check in the register. "My daughter is a big fan."

"Maybe she can stop by Rivers some time, and we can have a lovely chat," Brianne says, smiling.

The owner smiles. "I'll let her know you said that. If you don't mind, could I get a picture with you two?"

Nowell shakes his head and takes a step closer to the shop owner. "We would prefer...if you didn't tell anyone we were here." He crosses his arms and inches closer to the owner. "We really want to have a bit of privacy for the next couple of days if that's okay," he whispers. "The move has been hard on our son, and we think the fewer people following us around right now the better."

The owner is silent for a while, then says, "Of course, of course. I would really appreciate an autograph of some sort, though." He laughs. "My daughter will kill me if she at least doesn't get that."

"Again," Brianne says, "if your daughter wants to talk to us then she can come to Rivers and see us."

"So, no autograph?"

Nowell dangles the key to the sports yacht, and he and Brianne begin to walk away. "Look no further than the check." They then walk outside and get in their car. Brianne takes her shades off.

"I hate when you use Toby as an excuse like that."

Nowell takes his phone out and looks at a map, zooming out. "He's used us before to get what he wants. I don't see the harm in using him."

"He's just a kid, and do you blame him?"

"I don't blame anyone for anything," Nowell says. "People are gonna do whatever makes them happy, and Toby is no different." He looks at Brianne. "You and I are no different." He leans over to Brianne and shows her his phone. "You can drive the car over here, and I'll take the yacht and meet you there."

"You don't want to at least call Toby and tell him not to

worry about us? We can lie and say we're talking to a label or something."

Nowell shakes his head. "He wouldn't believe that. Either that or he'll think we don't care about him anymore. Look, Bri, he's fourteen. I'm sure he'll be happy to see us gone when he wakes up. It's just gonna be for today, and honestly, he's probably going to be gone all day with his friends anyway."

Brianne sighs and puts her shades back on. "Okay."

Nowell kisses her on the cheek. "I'm gonna share my location with you, just in case you get lost." He starts to get out of the car. "I love you," he says and then closes the door.

"Sure you do," Brianne says, cranking the car.

When Toby woke up in Rivers, he was confused by his parents' absence, but he didn't linger too long. Sitting at the kitchen table, eating a bowl of cereal, he tries calling each of his friends, but no one will answer. "Fuck this," he says. He gets up and puts his unfinished bowl of cereal in the sink and goes upstairs to brush his teeth and get dressed. He then walks to Seth and Eric's house. Toby knocks on the front door and is greeted by Eric.

"Oh," Eric says. "Hey, dude. It might not be a good idea to be here, right now."

"I'm sorry," Toby says. "I just tried calling all of you guys, and no one answered, so I came to check on you all."

"Thanks," Eric says awkwardly. "Listen"—he rubs the back of his head—"Bridgette told us all what happened yesterday. Seth kinda wants to kill you, right now, and I think Bridgette hates you."

"She doesn't hate me."

"You pushed her into a literal pigpen with mud and shit, dude. I'd hate you if you did that with me."

Toby sighs. "Look, I didn't push Bridgette, alright? She grabbed me, so I grabbed her, and we both fell."

"It doesn't matter, dude," Eric says. "Tensions are high, okay? Seth and Bridgette don't want to talk to you, and Chris and I can't talk to you because we'll look like dicks. Just give it a week and everything will be peachy."

Toby takes a step forward. "Can I *please* try to explain myself?"

Eric sighs. "Goddammit, fine. Follow me."

The two go inside, and Toby follows Eric to the living room. The other three friends are sitting on the couch watching television.

"Hey, Eric," Seth says, "who was at the door? You were out there for a long time."

"See for yourself," Eric says. He walks into his room and closes the door.

Seth turns around, sees Toby, and advances toward him. He pushes Toby into the wall. "What the fuck do you think you're doing here?"

"I was just trying to..."

"No!" Seth yells. He points toward the front door. "Get the fuck out of my house, you freak!"

"Can you please just let me apologize?"

"You had your chance to apologize yesterday, and you didn't. So"—he grabs Toby by the arm and throws him out the front door—"stay the fuck away from us." He slams the door, and Toby walks back home, holding back tears the whole way.

THAT NIGHT on the sports yacht, Nowell and Brianne are already on their third bottle of alcohol. They laugh and dance until an alarm on Brianne's phone goes off.

"Oh shit," she says. She takes a swig and taps Nowell on the chest. "We should get back. I want Toby to go to sleep knowing we're home."

"Why can't we spend the night here?" Nowell asks, kissing Brianne hard on the forehead. "Remember what you used to say to me? Something about he can't see me this way. Now he can't see *us* this way, Bri. We're both accountable."

"I don't want to sleep out here in the middle of nowhere."

"It's not the middle of nowhere," Nowell says, turning off the music. "If anything happens, I could send Waterston a drop so he can see where we are."

"He's so sad," Brianne says after another sip.

"We're all sad. I wasn't happy a day of my fucking life until I met you."

"Save the sweet talk, babe, I want to go home."

"Alright, alright."

Nowell goes to the wheel of the yacht and searches 'Rivers' into his 'maps' app on his phone. He starts the route and begins to ride toward the city, going 80 miles an hour. After about twenty minutes of driving, his phone dies.

"Shit," Nowell says. He throws his phone on the floor. "Bri! Phone's dead."

Brianne walks down to the wheel and Nowell with a small bag of cocaine. Nowell turns to her, sees the bag, and they both smile at each other.

"Can you open it for us, please?" Nowell asks, looking back at the water.

Brianne opens the bag and puts her index finger into it. She brings it up to Nowell's nose, and he snorts. He then puts one of his fingers in the bag and rubs some of the coke on his teeth.

"I don't know where Toby got this stuff, but it's good shit," Nowell says.

Brianne sits down on the floor and pours the rest of the coke out. She sniffs her share and when she comes back up says, "You've always been a lightweight with this stuff. Remember when you and Elisha would..."

"Pass me another drink, will you, Bri?"

Brianne gets up and hugs Nowell from behind. "No, sir, I can't let you drink and drive. Not without giving me a kiss. She turns him to his side, and they both begin the kiss, Nowell occasionally peeping his eye open to see where they're going. Things quickly go out of hand, and the couple get on the floor, Nowell keeping one hand on the gas pedal.

"It's a straight shot," he says.

The two continue to kiss, more passionately, more drunkenly. What could've been two or twenty minutes later, the sports yacht crashes into land, and Nowell and Brianne stumble onto the shore and black out.

7

ELECTRIC FEEL

Meanwhile, Toby is sitting in silence in his room. He's been looking out his window ever since he made it back home and hasn't eaten dinner. His stomach growls for the umpteenth time, but he ignores it again. The doorbell rings throughout the house. Toby looks toward his door, confused by who might be here this late. After a minute of silence, the doorbell rings again, and Toby heads downstairs. He opens the door and sees Bridgette. She's wearing a lavender shirt and light blue pajama pants that are decorated with unicorns.

"Hi," Bridgette says quietly.

"Um, hey," Toby says, confused.

"Can I come in for a little while?"

"Yeah, sure." Bridgette comes inside, and Toby closes the door. She stands in the middle of the floor.

"Thanks," she says, facing Toby with her arms crossed.

"No prob. Uh, do you want to go up to my room or?"

Bridgette shakes her head. "No, I'll make this quick."

"O-okay."

Bridgette sighs. "I appreciate you coming over to apologize, I do, but I'm sorry, Toby, I just can't trust you anymore."

Toby puts his hands in the pockets of his shorts. "That's understandable."

"And it's frustrating because I *want* to trust you, because, weirdly, I think you're a good person. And it doesn't make any sense to me because sometimes you're so *clearly* not."

"I'm sorry."

"No," Bridgette says, "don't be sorry. You can't help it, I guess. I mean, at first, I thought you wanted to demolish a building because of some weird way of getting back at your parents. But no one seriously thinks that, you know? I think maybe you're just broken."

"Why are you telling me this?"

Bridgette grabs her head out of frustration. "I don't know. I just felt compelled to come talk to you." She crosses her arms again. "Maybe I feel bad for you?"

"Why would you feel bad for me?" Toby says. "You barely even know me."

"There's so much about you, about anyone, that you don't even know yourself. I...I'm sorry for making you uncomfortable at the petting zoo. And I'm sorry that Seth treated you so shitty. And I'm sorry that I took away the few friends you had." Bridgette sniffles. "I know it's not completely my fault, but we, *I*, could've handled this much better. And I'm sorry."

"Well," Toby says, looking at his feet. "Thank you. I'm sorry for being a knob."

Bridgette laughs to herself, briefly covering her mouth. "A knob. No, Seth is a major knob. I can't believe he literally threw you out of his house."

Toby looks back up at Bridgette. "It hurt."

Bridgette's eyes widen. "Oh, did he bruise you or anything? I'm so sorry, Toby, I really am."

"No," Toby says, avoiding eye contact. "I, uh, can't believe I'm telling you this, but, I..." Toby's eyes water, and he starts to sniff. "I, um, you know what? Never mind." He walks to the door and opens it. "Thank you for coming over. It's really kind of you."

Bridgette walks over to the door and closes it. She faces Toby. "No, it was brave of you to come and apologize to me first. Not a lot of guys our age are mature enough to do something like that," she says almost to herself, "Seth sure isn't."

"It's just," Toby says, "I'm just so alone. I've felt alone my whole stupid life, and I finally felt normal for once. And I fucked it up. Because that's all I do. I fucked up making friends, I fucked up trying to buy a stupid fucking store, and I fucked up my parents' life. They left everything because of me. Maybe I'm not broken. Maybe I just break everything I touch."

Toby begins to sob, and Bridgette hugs him. "It's okay, Toby," Bridgette says, comforting him. "We're all broken." Toby looks up at Bridgette, wiping away his tears. Bridgette kisses him softly on the lips and walks out the door.

That was Toby's first kiss.

BRIANNE WAKES up on the shore, sand all over her face. She hears light footsteps coming toward her, and a beam of light gets her in the eye. A middle-aged woman, around 5' 4" and slender, crouches down to her.

"Oh my god," the woman says. "Are you alright?" She raises Brianne up and does her best to support her with her shoulder.

"What happened?" Brianne says.

"It looks like you crashed your speedboat there onto the shore."

Brianne looks around quickly but then drops to her knees, vomiting. When she's done, she asks, "Where's Nowell?"

"Who?" the woman says.

"My husband," Brianne says, then spits. "Where's my husband?"

The woman raises her flashlight and searches for Nowell. She crouches down to Brianne again, putting her hand on her shoulder. "You stay right here, love. I'm gonna go look for your husband." She stands and walks farther along the shore. Brianne stares at her vomit in the sand and begins to weep, holding herself. After a couple of minutes, the woman returns with Nowell. After spotting Brianne, Nowell runs to her and gets down on the ground with her. Brianne begins to cry harder, and they both hug.

The woman stands idly by while the couple has their moment. She eventually says, "We need to get you two to some shelter, clean you up." She waves her arm. "Walk with me to my house just off the shore, and I'll take care of you both."

Nowell and Brianne stand, and the three walk across the sandy shore. After about fifteen minutes, they reach a tiny wooden house and go inside. The woman turns on a light switch and escorts Nowell and Brianne to a couch in the living room.

"You two wait here while I get you a glass of water." The woman goes into her kitchen, takes a glass out of a cabinet, and gets water from the faucet. She then returns to the living room. "Here," she says, handing the glass to Brianne.

"Thank you," Brianne says. She takes a sip of water and

passes the glass to Nowell. "Thank you so much for helping us."

The woman sits on the couch across the room. "Oh, no problem at all. I'm just happy I haven't taken my medicine yet. Otherwise, I might've found you two in the morning."

"No, really," Brianne says, putting her hand on Nowell's knee. "Words cannot express how grateful we are." She turns to Nowell. "Isn't that right, sweetie?"

"Thank you," Nowell says gruffly. He starts coughing and drinks some more water.

The woman gets up. "I have a spare room upstairs for the two of you. I'll start a shower for you and get some clothes. I didn't catch your name, dear."

"Brianne," Brianne says. "Thank you so much."

"Absolutely, Brianne. I live here by myself, so you'll have some women's clothes, though they will be a little tight. Nowell, you'll have to make do with the same."

"I'll take anything but what I have on now," Nowell says, placing the glass of water on a nearby end table.

"Oh no, I got it," the woman says. She walks across the room, picks up the glass, and starts to walk up the stairs. "I'll go start your shower, now. You two just wait here." She goes up the stairs for a few minutes, then calls for Nowell and Brianne to come up. In the bathroom, the woman tells them, "I have the water nice and warm for you and have your clothes and towels here." She nods to the clothes and towels laying on the kitchen sink. "The spare room is just down the hall, and my room is right here beside the bathroom. I'm going to go to bed, but I won't be taking my sleep medication tonight. If either of you needs anything, just come and knock on my door."

Nowell and Brianne thank the woman. The woman

begins to leave, but before she does, Brianne asks for her name.

"Janie," she says. She closes the bathroom door behind her.

Nowell and Brianne shower together for thirty minutes, the warm water feeling like a much-needed hug. They dry off and put the clothes on, which were indeed tight. They leave their dirty clothes on the floor, deciding they won't bother Janie about what to do with them. They then go into the spare bedroom, close the door, and get under the covers.

Brianne passes out in less than five minutes and sleeps soundly into the night. Nowell, however, stays awake. After about an hour, he takes his arm from around Brianne and sneaks out of the bedroom. He quietly closes the door, then walks down to Janie's room, opening the door and entering. Janie is sitting in bed, wearing pajama shorts and nothing else.

"Your voice is softer," Nowell says, standing by the door.

"Took you long enough to come see me," Janie says.

Nowell walks over to the bed and sits beside her. He stares into her eyes and whispers, "What the hell do you think you're doing here? And whose house is this?"

"I came looking for you, Nowell," Janie says confidently. "Did you actually think you could hide from me? You haven't been doing a very good job, you know."

"How long have you been here?"

"Doesn't matter."

"Did Elisha set you up here?"

"What if he did?" Janie asks. "You've never cared to take care of me in the past."

"That's not true," Nowell says.

"I haven't seen you since '96, at least not in person.

Hadn't heard your voice until I called you a few months ago."

"What do you want from me? Why won't you just leave me and my family alone?"

Janie looks at Nowell with faux shock in her eyes. "Family? You think you can convince me you give a single shit about family?" She leans closer to him. "I *know* you, Nowell."

Nowell looks down at the bed. "I asked you what you want from me."

"I want you to give me another chance."

Nowell looks into Janie's eyes. "Another chance at what? I have Brianne and Toby, and you have your life. Don't ruin mine."

Janie looks down at Nowell's crotch and back up at him. "I hope *you* haven't gotten soft," she says softly.

Nowell stares at Janie for a few seconds, then puts his hand under her shorts.

Janie smiles. "Did you miss me?"

"Shut up," Nowell says. He begins to suck on Janie's neck and moves his other hand into her shorts. She pushes his face away.

"She'll find out if you do that."

"She's a fucking idiot," Nowell says. He yanks Janie's shorts off and turns her around on her knees. He then undresses and adds, "Just a pretty, conceited idiot."

8

HEAVY METAL DRUMMER

The next morning, Toby wakes up and sees he has a text from Seth asking to come hang out. Toby texts him back saying he'll be there in an hour. Toby gets out of bed, stretches, and goes to the bathroom to brush his teeth. While doing so, he hears the front door open. He spits into the sink and walks out of the bathroom.

"Mom? Dad?"

"Toby?" Brianne calls from downstairs. Nowell closes the door behind her, and Toby meets them down the stairs.

"Where were you guys?"

Nowell sighs. "We had an important meeting with the mayor yesterday, and he had us talk to all sorts of people."

"That took up the whole day?" Toby asks. "Just a couple of meetings?"

"No, not a couple of meetings," Nowell says. "We had to drive to a few different towns and talk to these people personally. For confidentiality purposes."

"One of our new business partners gave us a new car," Brianne exclaims.

Toby raises an eyebrow. "So, we have two now?

"Um, no," Nowell says.

"We donated our old one to charity," Brianne says.

"Which charity?" Toby asks, crossing his arms.

"Well," Nowell begins.

"Never mind," Toby says, putting his hands in his pockets. "I'm happy to have you back."

Brianne smiles. "We're happy to see you, too, sweetheart." She walks to the kitchen. "So, how was your day yesterday?" she asks as she sits at the kitchen table.

"Oh, uh," Toby starts. He walks to the kitchen, and Nowell heads up the stairs. "Nothing, really. Stayed here, mostly." He sits across from Brianne.

"You didn't hang out with your friends?"

"Oh, I did," Toby says. "Kinda. My friend Bridgette came over."

Brianne perks up. She leans closer, elbows on the table. "What did you guys do?"

"We just talked."

"What about?"

"About people," Toby says. "About how people don't really know themselves."

"Don't really know themselves?"

"Yeah, like, how everyone is kinda broken inside, you know?"

Brianne leans back in her chair. "No, I don't. Do you and your little friend, Bridgette, talk about that kind of stuff a lot?"

"No. We just kinda did last night."

"She came over last night? What the hell kind of girl is Bridgette? Coming over to your house at night."

"Mom, we just talked, I swear." Toby stands and heads out of the kitchen.

"Where are you going?" Brianne asks firmly. "To see

Bridgette?"

"No," Toby says, stopping. "I'm gonna go see her boyfriend, Seth."

Brianne grabs Toby's arm, and they look each other in the eyes. "Be back for dinner. No later, and *definitely* no sooner. Your father and I need to rest today."

"You guys didn't do that last night at the mayor's house or whatever?"

Brianne lets go of Toby's arm. "Just go out and play."

"Okay. Bye."

"I love you, too."

Toby goes out the front door, and Brianne goes upstairs to her bedroom. Nowell is lying on the bed, initially looking at the ceiling, but he leans up once Brianne enters the room.

"Is he gone?"

Brianne closes the door and locks it. "Hopefully for the rest of the day, yes. Did you know that he's friends with a girl, and she came over last night?"

"Do you think they did anything?"

"I don't think so. But she sounds like a bad influence."

"How?"

Brianne sits on the bed. "He said the only thing they did last night was talk. Talk about being broken or some kind of weird shit kids do these days."

"Why would they talk about that?"

"I don't know, Nowell. That's just what he told me." Brianne pauses and looks at the mirror on their bedroom door. "I'm worried about him."

Nowell lies back down on the bed. "Toby's fine. He's a smart kid."

"Do you think so?"

"Of course, I do. Am I not supposed to?"

"That's not what I mean, Nowell."

"Why are you worried about him having a conversation with some girl?"

"Toby's very impressionable."

"Everyone under the age of twenty-five is impressionable, Bri."

"Toby hasn't had many friends, though." Brianne gasps and looks at Nowell. "Do you think he's on drugs? He had the bag we took from him."

"You think Toby's on drugs?"

"He could be. That would explain him talking about being broken. Maybe he needs another fix."

"What is there to fix? Toby's fine."

"Or maybe he's unhappy," Brianne says. "He seemed fine to me, but maybe he misses home."

Nowell leans up again. "He *is* home, Bri. Rivers is a great place for him. There's an excellent college here, and the high school's not that bad."

"I *know*, Nowell. I read the same shit you did. I'm just saying that maybe we need to sit and talk with him. Ask him if he's okay." Brianne puts her face in her hands. "Oh God, I grabbed him by the arm before he left." She looks at Nowell. "What if he hates me? Hates us?"

"Then he's a normal teenager. I think you need to take a nap."

"No, I don't. We should tell him what's been going on. Let him feel closer to us."

Nowell scoffs and sits on the bed, legs crossed. "So he can actually hate us? Look down on us and be disappointed? He can't know what we did yesterday, Bri. At the most, we just tell him that we needed some alone time."

"Not yesterday, Nowell." Brianne sighs. "Forget I said anything."

Nowell gets off the bed and walks over to the closet. He

reaches for the top shelf, moves some boxes, and grabs a tiny bag of marijuana. He faces Brianne. "No, let's talk."

"You want to start a band," Toby says. He and the gang, minus Bridgette, are sitting at a round table in Seth and Eric's basement. "I thought you guys hated me now?"

"Well," Seth says, "I never liked you. Besides, this was more of a Chris idea, anyways." He points at Chris, who nods.

"Right," Chris says. "We already got the framework done. I play guitar, Eric on bass, and Seth on drums. Eric was on vocals—"

"But I can't sing for shit," Eric finishes.

"So, I wanted to ask you to join us," Chris says. "Just to sing, of course."

"Yeah," Toby says. "Sure. Um, thanks for including me."

"Besides," Seth says, "we can probably use you to bribe someone to sign us."

"What he means to say is that because of you being... who you are, you might have some natural musical prowess."

"I don't think I have touched an instrument since I was six," Toby says. "Or write a line of poetry."

"Did your mom actually write all the lyrics for Lonely Souls?" Eric asks, arms crossed behind his head.

"From what I'm told, yeah."

"Hmm."

The door to the basement opens, and Bridgette walks in. She closes the door behind her and walks down the stairs. "Seth," she says, "I want to break up." She gestures toward the rest of the group. "And I don't think we should all hang out for a while."

Seth gets up. "Is there something wrong?"

"Yes," Bridgette says, picking at her wristband. "But in order to make changes you have to start with yourself, and I'm making that move now."

"What are you talking about?"

"I'd rather not say."

"No," Seth exclaims. "You made the effort to come over and announce to all of us that you and I are breaking up. So, you can tell us all why you don't want to be around anymore." He looks at Toby and back at Bridgette. "Is it because of him? You told me he apologized to you."

"You told him about last night?" Toby asks Bridgette.

Bridgette and Seth's eyes light up. "What the hell is this about last night?" Seth asks.

"Seth," Bridgette begins.

"No, you don't get to walk in here and…"

"It's both of you, okay!" Bridgette screams.

The room gets quiet.

Bridgette continues. "Seth, I need someone who is patient, calm, and kind. After what you did to Toby yesterday, and even now with how you're acting, I don't think that's the kind of person you are." She looks at Toby. "And, Toby, I wish I could help you, but you need some more growing up to do." She looks at the whole group. "I'm sorry, but I feel uncomfortable with being around you guys, and maybe I'll be back in your friend group. For now, though, I need to focus on myself. I'm sorry."

Bridgette walks out of the basement and out the front door of the house. Seth slaps his hand on the table.

"Damn it! I can't believe this shit!"

"Seth," Toby says, "you should go after her."

Seth shakes his head. "No, fuck that." He waves his hand at the others. "And fuck this, too. Chris, I'm sorry, but I think this band idea is stupid, and I *really* don't like you, Toby. I quit." He walks out of the basement and slams the door behind him. The three boys look at each other, sharing their confusion at what just happened.

"So," Eric says, "you know how to play the drums?"

9

NOT JUST MONEY

"I think we should spend some time apart," Brianne says, taking a hit of a joint.

Nowell sits on the floor, looking up at her on the bed. "Is it because of me, or is it for less publicity?"

Brianne passes the joint to Nowell. "We're at a point where it's because of everything, Nowell. I need to be alone."

"For how long?"

"Time will tell."

"Why have you always been so dramatic, Bri? 'Time will tell.' Why can't you say you don't know?" Nowell takes a puff, then passes it back.

"I don't know."

They sit in silence for a few moments.

"Where will I go?" Nowell asks.

"I'm sure you know a place. You always find a way to be where you need to be."

"Is that disdain?"

"Shut up, Nowell."

Nowell stands up. "I'll...see you when it's time, then." He walks over to kiss Brianne, but she stops him.

"Don't."

Nowell nods, leaves the room, and goes outside the house. He walks with a purpose to the wealthier side of Rivers, knowing exactly where he wants to go. He walks up to the front door of a two-story yellow house and rings the doorbell. After a few moments, Elisha answers the door. He leans on the doorframe.

"I started to think you weren't going to come visit me," Elisha says.

"I need to stay here for a while," Nowell says. "I hope that's okay."

"Sure," Elisha says, standing upright. "Any time. But how long is a while, if you don't mind me asking?"

"Time will tell."

Meanwhile, Brianne is sitting in her bedroom, looking at the mirror on her door and weeping. The front door opens, and she hears Toby call out for his parents.

"Goddammit," Brianne says. She squishes the joint with her foot into the rug and stares at her bare feet. Toby comes up the stairs, still calling for his parents but quieter now. He knocks on the bedroom door and peeps in.

"Oh, I'm..." Toby starts, but he walks in after seeing his mother distressed. "Are you okay, Mom?"

"I'm fine, thank you."

"Where's Dad?"

Brianne looks up at Toby, her eyes bloodshot. "Your father is going to be away for a while."

"Are you guys getting a divorce?"

"No," Brianne says confidently. "I just need to be alone, that's all."

"Oh, okay."

"What did you want, Toby?"

"I'm sorry?"

"You were calling for me and your father," Brianne says, getting up from the bed. She crosses her arms. "What did you want?"

"Oh, uh, my friends and I started a band today."

"Well, that's good. You don't know how to play any instruments, though. You asked to take those guitar lessons years ago and gave up after a month, remember?"

"I'm gonna be singing, Mom."

"You can sing?"

"They can't, so they asked me."

"I guess you gotta work with what you got," Brianne says. She begins to walk to the bathroom in her room.

"That's, um, actually what I wanted to talk to you and Dad about," Toby says, taking a step forward.

Brianne stops, one hand on the bathroom doorknob. "What do you mean, Toby?" she asks quietly.

"Well, my friends don't really have the best instruments. I mean, they're good and we can totally work with them. But they could be better... the instruments."

Brianne waves her hand. "What are you trying to say?" She clearly looks frustrated, and Toby pauses before continuing.

"I was wondering if I can have some money to buy us some newer instruments. Maybe even some equipment."

"Do you even know what the *fuck* you're saying?" Brianne yells.

Toby starts to walk out of the bedroom. "Okay, sorry I asked."

"No," Brianne says. She quickly gets in front of Toby and slams the bedroom door. "You have the nerve to come in here and ask me for more money? The money that *I* worked for?"

"You and Dad worked for it."

Brianne slaps Toby and points a finger at him. "You watch what you say to me, Toby, or so help me I will take your life like you took mine nearly fifteen goddamn years ago!" She pushes him onto the bed and stands over him. "All you do is take whatever you have for granted. Your father and I ended our lives because of you. And what have you shown for it? You wasted our money with music lessons, you stole money from our safe, and now you want money to buy these random kids you met some equipment that you don't know a single fucking thing about."

"I didn't take money from the safe, Mom," Toby says, terrified.

"Oh, but you did. Before we moved here *and* on the first fucking day we moved to this shithole! Your father told me before that I'm paranoid, but I went in the safe, and the money was *not* how I left it."

"I didn't take any money, Mom," Toby says, leaning up. "I went in the safe, and I'm sorry for that, but I didn't take anything."

"Then please tell me what the fuck you were doing in our safe," Brianne says, taking a step back.

"I took some out because I wanted to make an investment in the record store here in Rivers."

"An investment?"

"Yes."

"And it didn't go well, so you brought the money that you stole and put it back in our safe?"

"*Yes*, Mom," Toby says, beginning to cry. "I'm sorry."

"So it was you that destroyed all of that stuff in the record store downtown?"

Toby stops. "How...how do you know that?"

"Because Mayor Waterston told me and your father about it. When we were talking about the crime in Rivers."

Brianne runs her hands through her hair. "You little thieving shit, *you* did that. Why on *earth* would you do that?"

"Why are you talking to me like this?"

"Answer my goddamn question, you entitled little zit!"

"I just want someone to pay attention to me, okay? Maybe you and Dad can try actually *talking* to me."

Brianne squats on the floor, her hand in a praying position. Toby looks at her, unsure what to do. "How much money did you take?"

"I told you, I didn't take any money," Toby says, his words unclear from his sobbing.

Brianne hugs herself. "I believe you. How much money did you take to the record store owner to make your fake investment."

"$250, 000."

Brianne gets up, opens her closet door, then the safe. She opens the safe and says, "It's unfortunate that the record store owner didn't sell out your identity. Maybe this could've been avoided." She pauses. "Maybe it's for the best."

Toby looks at Brianne on the floor. "What are you doing, Mom?"

Brianne starts taking money out of the safe. "Go get a duffle bag from your room. Now!"

Toby gets up and runs to get the same bag he brought to the record store. He returns to Brianne, who snatches it from him. She starts shoving cash into the bag, counting quietly to herself. When she's done, she zips up the bag, stands up, and shoves it into Toby's arms.

"I'm going to make an investment," Brianne says. She walks toward Toby, who slowly walks backwards to the door. "I'm giving you the chance to *make* something of yourself. To give your father and me a reason to pay attention to you." She points her finger again. "You are going to take this money and get the fuck out of this house. I don't care where you stay, but you won't be living here. Use that money to make your stupid band thing work out, and don't come back here until you're worthy."

Toby bumps his back on the doorknob. Brianne gets down a little to be at eye level with him. "And if you tell anyone what happened here or what you're really doing, I promise you I will have you killed. Your father and I know people, and if I don't do it myself, someone will get you, mark my words." She pushes Toby, and he runs out of the house.

Not having anywhere else to go, and partly because of the words his mother just screamed at him, Toby goes straight to Seth and Eric's house. He knocks on the door, and Eric answers the door again.

"Woah," Eric says, "are you okay?"

"I need to talk to your parents," Toby says, his face still wet.

"About what, dude? What the hell do you have that bag again for?"

"I have money in it. I need to talk to your parents so I can live here."

"Why do you want to live here?" Eric asks. "What happened at your house?"

"My parents loved the idea of us being in a band. So, they gave me this money so I can pay your parents to let me stay here and for us to do whatever we can for the band."

Eric stares at Toby. "Are you serious?"

"100%."

A giant smile goes across Eric's face. "Awesome! Seth's gonna be pissed that he quit once he learns this. Um, my parents aren't here, but you can come on in. I'm gonna call Chris."

Eric turns and disappears inside. Toby comes into the house, closes the door behind him, and walks into the living room. He sits on a couch and sets the duffle bag on the coffee table in front of it. The news on the television drones on about a mysterious yacht that crashed in a nearby town. Toby grabs the remote off the coffee table and turns the television off. He stares at himself on the black screen.

10

THE SOUND OF SETTLING

A few days later, despite what she had told him, Brianne calls Nowell to come back home. She had spent her days alone in their mansion away from the rest of Rivers, only ever going outside to sit on the porch and smoke. The inside of their home remained largely the same as Nowell and Toby left it, including both Toby and Brianne's closet doors being open from their last encounter. When Nowell comes home, he is shocked at how unchanged the house is. He is still confused about why Brianne called for him to come home.

"Did you go to his house?" Brianne asks, putting a cigarette out in an ashtray in the living room.

"I did," Nowell says. "Where's Toby?"

"I kicked him out," Brianne says. "He admitted to trying to take money from us. So, I let him have it and told him not to come back."

"Do you think he'll tell anyone what's wrong?"

"You're his father, and you didn't even ask me what happened exactly."

They stand in silence, the only sound being the birds chirping outside. Nowell speaks first.

"Why did you call me?"

"With Toby gone, and you going over to Elisha's, I think it's time for us to make the fourth album."

Nowell, surprised, asks, "You don't think that will look bad? We haven't exactly finished *raising* Toby. Also, he's not here anymore. People are going to be wondering where our son is."

"Our son came home asking for money to start a band before I kicked him out."

"A band," Nowell asks. "With who? Some random kids on the street?"

"His so-called friends."

"Do you think he's staying with one of them?"

"If I had to guess, he probably gave one of their parents some cash to live with them, yes."

"How much money did you give him?"

"$250,000," Brianne says, taking a seat on a couch. "I told him to not come back until his band is successful. If he succeeds, then we can talk in interviews about how our son, who we stopped making music for, has inherited some of his parents' skills. If he doesn't, we can use our status once we announce our return to bring attention to his band."

"When should we release an album then?"

"We should give Toby time since he has no idea what he's doing. In the meantime, I want us to talk to Elisha so we can have different marketing strategies planned just in case any issues come up."

"And why do you think Elisha will want us back?"

"People love nostalgia these days. Nowell, the people who listened to Lonely Souls are now fifteen, twenty years older. Even though it was mostly our talent, Elisha was a key part of our success. We write the songs, balance out the old and new, and he does the business side of things—save for telling us what doesn't work, occasionally."

"Where do we start?" Nowell asks as he sits beside Brianne. "Musically. Do we work with some old songs, start fresh, or...?"

"The first thing we need to do is go to Elisha's together and talk this all out. Tell him everything and see where we go from here." Brianne looks Nowell in the eye. "What did you two do while you were there?"

Nowell adjusts on the couch, inhaling, and then turns to Brianne and exhales. "We just talked about when we were younger. I told him about Toby since he's never met him. I told him about what we're doing here."

"What did he think?"

"That we need to grow up."

"Well," Brianne says, standing up and facing Nowell, "after we talk to him, the only place we'll be going is up. Just like before." She crouches down to Nowell's knees, rubs them, and looks up at Nowell. "We will *not* be forgotten, never again."

SETH KNOCKS on the front door twice before Bridgette opens it. She sees him and begins to close the door.

"Wait," Seth says, putting his foot in the door. "Ow."

"What do you want, Seth?"

"I wanted to talk to you," Seth says, taking his foot from the door. "About us."

"Ugh," Bridgette says. "I'm not getting back together with you. Now, if you'll excuse me, I have some lines to go over." She begins to close the door again, but Seth grabs it.

"Wait, wait, wait. I know you're not gonna get back with me and that's fine. I'm not here for that."

Bridgette opens the door all the way. "Then what are you doing here?"

"I just want to ask you if you can put a good word in for me with your dad."

"For his comedy club? I've never heard you make a remotely humorous joke ever."

"I know, I know," Seth says. "I just need...something, okay? You left me, and I think Chris's band idea is stupid..."

"You haven't even *tried* Chris's band idea," Bridgette interrupts, annoyed.

"I know I haven't, but Toby is in the band now, and he keeps coming over to... He's staying at our house, Bee."

Bridgette shakes her head. "Don't call me that. What do you mean, like, he's staying there full time?"

Seth nods. "Yes. The rich bastard left after you broke up with me and came back later with the freaking money he had for the record store. It was in the same bag and everything. And he's fucking paying my parents to let him stay there and make music because he said his parents wanted to make an investment or some shit, I don't know, Bridgette. It's fucking insane, and I need some way to get out of the house for the rest of the summer, at least, and probably while school's going, too."

Following a quiet, "Oh my god," Bridgette covers her face in frustration. She eventually sighs and says, "Okay, fine. I'll ask my dad if you can work at the comedy club. I'll even tell him you're funny, and *maybe* he'll let you perform."

Seth grabs Bridgette's hand and shakes it rapidly. "Thank you so much," he says before Bridgette yanks her hand away.

"No prob, dude. Seriously, though, I need to go over

some lines." Bridgette starts to go into the house, then stops. She looks at Seth. "Was this your first solution? To come to me and become a comedian?"

"Yeah, pretty much."

Bridgette smirks. "Then you'll do alright."

IN SETH and Eric's basement, Toby, Chris, and Eric are sitting at the round table. They haven't made much progress the past few days as Toby had been busy negotiating his living situation with Seth and Eric's parents. The deal is that Toby will pay a flat $1000 a month as his way of rent. Their monthly mortgage payment is $1400, and Toby gives them an extra $400 as a 'confidentiality fee.' Toby sleeps in the basement (he bought a futon the day after he was kicked out by Brianne) and he has been slowly buying clothes to wear. He keeps the few clothes he has in a tall hamper that Eric let him use.

"We need a drum machine," Chris says. "Maybe we can get someone later to play drums live, but to be safe, we need a drum machine. I don't think Toby will be able to sing and play drums at the same time."

"Okay," Toby says, writing it down in a notebook. "What type of genre are we going for?"

"Well, we've kinda been doing a hard rock type thing."

"No," Toby says, "we're not doing that. We need to do something more ear grabby, more commercial, but not literally pop music."

"I mean, we can try, but the songs we have written now are hard rock songs."

Toby snaps his fingers. "We can make it punky. Three teenage boys from a college town making punk music."

"How are we going to rewrite our rock songs into punk songs?" Eric asks.

"Speed it up, I don't know. But we'll figure it out. I think the only ways to go about this are either punk music or an indie sound. Especially if we start to gain a following. If people see that the son of Lonely Souls, the soul duo, started making loud abrasive music then that will get some attention. But it'll also work if the music is more mellow."

"Punk then," Chris says. Toby makes a note. "What's the name going to be?"

"Of the band?" Toby asks.

"Yes, of the band. If we're trying to be more commercial then we need a commercial name."

"Well, then we need sex appeal."

"For teenage boys?" Eric asks.

"We won't be teenagers forever," Toby says.

"So, sex appeal name for a punk band from the son of Lonely Souls," Chris says.

The group was silent for five minutes before Toby snapped his fingers, his face showing an 'A-ha' moment.

"A Taste of Tongue."

11

LOVE THEME FROM KISS

In September of the following year, Nowell and Brianne complete production on their new album. Instead of announcing the news via the Internet, the couple is advised by Elisha to announce the album's completion on the local show 'Good Morning, Rivers'. Elisha schedules them for an interview to talk about what the couple has done during their nearly year and a half tenure in Rivers.

"You have to cap off the interview with the announcement of your new album," Elisha says. "Talk about your relationship with the mayor, how you've decreased crime, and then talk about the local music scene. Mention me and say how being in Rivers reignited your passion for music and that my being here was a matter of coincidence."

Nowell and Brianne do just that in their morning interview on Good Morning, Rivers. "We're very passionate people," Nowell says, sipping from a cup of coffee. "When we saw what was trying to be hidden in the media, Bri and I knew we had to do something. Our relationship with Mayor Waterston hasn't been without its setbacks, but we're in a place now where we can all comfortably give suggestions and work together to help strengthen the community."

"I'm honestly surprised that he hasn't kicked us out," Brianne jokes, getting a chuckle from Nowell.

"Well," the interviewer says, "I'm not sure how much power Mayor Waterston actually has compared to you two. There are only about 25,000 residents in Rivers, give or take. I couldn't find any information past 2014. And Mayor Waterston claims to make about $49,000 a year. Sure, Lonely Souls hasn't released any music since 2000, but even now in 2017, *Biennial* sells like hotcakes. Not to mention the boost in sales you guys got last year upon moving to Rivers. A quick search online shows that you two combined have a net worth of $50 million."

"I can assure you we don't have that much money," Nowell says.

"Maybe not, but let me tell you what some residents of Rivers are thinking now. Now that the excitement is starting to die down about Lonely Souls moving here, many residents are starting to believe that the two of you have some control over the mayor. How can Mayor Waterston 'kick you out' of Rivers when you can easily take advantage of him monetarily?"

"We have no reason to use the mayor," Brianne says.

"No reason? Not even a week after you guys moved here, you were trying to implement a, some may argue, progressive strategy to reform the inmates of Rivers. Also, three months before relocating here, there was a controversy about you two that has mostly disappeared, yes, but is now slowly coming back into the public eye."

"I—" Nowell begins, but he is then interrupted.

"Lastly, your son, sixteen-year-old Toby Lewis-Green, started a band here not two months after moving here. A

Taste of Tongue is still rather small, but it has nevertheless been growing at a steady pace. Some residents believe that your son is a plant or a distraction from what you two are trying to escape. As your reason for leaving the spotlight nearly seventeen years ago was to focus on your son."

"This interview is over," Brianne says. "But before we go, we are choosing not to talk any further about these allegations because we've already talked about them in our new album, *Vestigial*. It's coming out in November, and if there's *anything* anyone needs to know, they will just have to listen to it. Come on, Nowell."

Nowell and Brianne leave the room.

THAT NIGHT, A Taste of Tongue are on stage performing their closing song: "Apocalyptic Love." The first song written by the band once Toby joined, the lyrics are simple, but the music goes at a breakneck pace for two minutes, with a crunchy guitar by Chris, chugging baselines from Eric, and a manic, yet soulful, vocal performance from Toby himself. The group uses a drum machine in their makeshift studio which is Toby's room. For live performances, they stick to being a three-piece, giving the band a unique sound.

Apocalyptic love has driven me crazy
Sex, then boredom is all that I know
When awake, I long to relive nightmares
At the end of each day, no home to go

OPTIMISM NEVER SOLVES problems
Only pessimists strive to survive
When did we run out of morals?
I answer this question on sleepless nights

. . .

I'm afraid of growing old
    Paying bills, making deals, what a wonderful lie
    Deceived to do what you've told
    A machine that bleeds all through life

I lost myself
    I do need help

THE CROWD of around a hundred people roars, and Toby thanks them and hopes they have a good night. The band exits through the back of the bar.

"I fucking hate that song," Toby says, closing the door behind him. The three boys walk to Toby's car, where they put the two guitars and amps in his trunk. They then get in the car, Eric in the backseat.

"You bitch about the lyrics every time we play it," Chris says, rubbing his forehead from frustration. "Either change them up or don't perform the song."

"The crowd loves that song," Toby says, beginning to drive. "We can't drop it because of my shitty lyrics."

"Well, maybe if you let us rework the words for you..." Eric says.

"No," Toby exclaims. "Whenever we make it big, we need to have each member do their one thing. It makes us stick out."

"That's stupid," Eric says, sighing.

"I don't care what you think," Toby says. "Chris, straight home?"

"Yes."

"We'll play it first next time. That'll drive them nuts."

"Right," Chris says.

Toby drives to Chris's house and drops him off. Before Chris closes the car door, Toby says, "When we get signed to a label, they'll tell us what to do."

"And when is that going to happen, Toby?" Chris asks. "We could've just *made* a label with the money you have."

"It *can't* be that way. We have to earn it. The son of Lonely Souls can't buy his way into relevance. Just like the son of Lonely Souls shouldn't have crap lyrics. Do you want your guitar?"

Chris shakes his head. "Leave it. I'll see you guys later." He closes the door and walks inside his house. Eric makes his way into the front seat.

"Seriously," Eric says, "when is all of this going to work out?"

"Soon," Toby says, pulling away. "I have a few ideas."

"I hope so," Eric says, putting his feet on the dash. "I feel like Seth is more successful with his silly stand-up sometimes."

"Seth's already failed at being more successful than I am," Toby says.

Seth was, however, proving to be more successful than A Taste of Tongue. After Bridgette put a good word in for him, Seth began working at the comedy club making schedules and cleaning up every night. Once school began last year, Seth asked Bridgette's father if he could start doing a set every week. Bridgette's father, Mr. Miller, declined, instead offering Seth the chance to introduce each comic.

Seth did this each weekend for several months, and then after the show was over, he would go in the office to work on schedules. He no longer cleaned since there was a new cleaning boy hired. By this time, Mr. Miller trusted Seth to close the club on his own. Seth would often start making himself drinks that way the lonesomeness of being in a dark and dusty office at night could be more bearable. By February 2017, Seth would drink about a fifth of bourbon a night, whether he was at work or at home.

At first, Seth had gotten drinks from the bar, but he believed that Mr. Miller was starting to grow suspicious. Then one day that February, Seth noticed Chris's uncle, Richard, at the comedy club. Seth watched him as each comic came onstage until Richard got up to exit. Seth followed him outside to ask Richard if there was any way he could buy alcohol from him. Richard agreed, of course, and every weekend he would bring Seth alcohol in exchange for money.

That Spring, Mr. Miller approached Seth and asked if he would like to start doing stand-up.

"The summer is coming up," Mr. Miller said. "So if you're any good, I'll have you perform every night when the time comes."

Seth agreed and began doing stand-up every weekend at the comedy club. The first few occasions were not the best —partly because of Seth's intoxication, but mostly because of simply not being very funny. Eventually, Seth hit his stride, writing jokes every night after school. By the time the summer started, the crowd would cheer for Seth to come onstage.

In June, Seth is suffering a bit of writer's block. After taking a seat after his set, Richard comes over to Seth so they can do their weekly deal. The two walk to the back of the club and stand by Seth's car.

"You were kinda rusty up there tonight, kid," Richard says.

Seth hands him the money and takes a brown bag. "I've

been having trouble coming up with some new material. It's hard since Mr. Miller has me up there every night now."

"Coming up with material," Richard asks. He smiles, reaches into his back pocket, and takes out a small bag with cocaine in it. "Whenever I need to be creative, I just take a sniff of this."

Seth takes a step back. "No, no, no. I think I just need to take a break or something."

Richard throws the bag at Seth's chest, and Seth catches it. "Just try it once. Take it before a show or before you write. I promise you'll see a difference. I'm gonna go back inside. It's too fucking hot out here for it to be nighttime."

As Richard walks away, Seth puts his bourbon in the car and sits in the front seat, looking at the tiny bag.

By the time September comes, he feels he couldn't live without it. When Toby and Eric come back home after their show, Seth is sleeping hard on the couch. On the coffee table in front of him, his phone is vibrating. Toby walks over to pick it up.

"It's Bridgette," Toby whispers to Eric.

"He hasn't talked to her in months."

"Probably butt-dialed him." Toby puts the phone back on the table and it continues to ring.

12

ACTION! NOT WORDS

Seth picks up the phone. It's the previous July, and the ringing wakes him up after a long, drunken sleep after work. Lying on the couch and not facing the coffee table, Seth lays the phone against his ear, not seeing who has called him. "Hello," he says, groggily.

"Hey. Did I wake you?" It's Bridgette.

Seth gets up quickly, the phone falling to the floor. He picks it up and answers, "Uh, yeah, but it's fine. What's up?"

"Not much. I have a commercial to shoot in a couple of hours."

"Oh cool," Seth says, standing up and wrapping his torso with a blanket. "What's it about?"

"It's a commercial for some kind of water with a bunch of minerals in it."

Seth is by the sink, getting water from the faucet. "That's cool. So, no offense, but are you calling me to talk to me about mineral water?" He takes a sip from the glass.

"Not exactly. The commercial is being shot at the Rivers Country Club, and my dad can't come with me. So, I was wondering if you'd like to come."

"To watch you film your commercial?"

"Yeah. I mean, not if you don't want to. There's golf and stuff there. Oh, and they're having a firework show tonight!"

Seth sits on the couch. "A firework show? For what?"

"It's the Fourth of July."

"Oh, right," Seth says, putting the cold glass of water to his head. "I, uh, was up late last night."

"So, do you wanna come?"

"Sure. Do I have to wear anything specific? I've never been to a country club."

"I guess wear a polo shirt and some shorts. And bring some swim trunks and a change of clothes. There's a pool if you wanna take a dip after the commercial is done."

"You said it's in a couple hours," Seth says. "Should I meet you there or...?"

"We'll meet each other there in about an hour. Don't be late, okay?"

"I won't be late."

"Thank you, Seth."

"Yeah."

Seth cleans up, packs a change of clothes, and drives to the Rivers Country Club. Bridgette is standing at the front gate as he pulls up. With a smile, she walks over to Seth's car as he rolls the window down.

"Mind if I get in?" Bridgette asks.

"Absolutely." Seth unlocks the car door, and Bridgette gets in.

"Because of the commercial and the Fourth of July celebration, they won't just have anyone come in today. We're gonna drive to the parking lot, and you can just follow me."

"Okay," Seth says. "So, um, how have you been?"

Bridgette looks at him energetically. "I'm good! I've been

really getting a groove on with my commercials. I've been making a killing, too."

"You really make that much money off commercials?"

"I'm making so much money that I'm seriously thinking about *just* doing commercials." Bridgette looks forward. "For example, today I'm making $600 just to film this one. I don't know how many takes it'll be, but still, it's $600. Plus, my dad made a deal where I'll make $2200 just to have the ad play online."

Seth whistles. "How much do you generally make from a commercial?"

"The least I've ever made from just filming one was like $300. But sometimes I get paid to rehearse with the other actors if there are any. I'm the sole actor in this commercial."

"I'm happy you've been successful," Seth says. He parks the car, and the two get out.

"I hear you've been doing well," Bridgette says. She flashes an ID card around her neck at a worker, and she and Seth walk through the entrance. "Dad told me you're actually funny now."

"That's what the audience thinks."

"I'm sure you are. But don't tell me any jokes, okay? I'll have to come see you sometime at the comedy club."

Seth stops and so does Bridgette. "What's wrong?" Bridgette asks.

"Thank you. For getting your dad to hire me."

"No probs, man. It really was—"

"I never thanked you," Seth interrupts. "I haven't talked to you since last year, and part of that was because I was bitter. But, thank you, Bee, for doing that."

Bridgette is silent for a few moments then says, "Of course." She then punches Seth in the arm, and he screams, then Bridgette says, "For a comedian, you seem pretty down.

And pale. After I'm done with my commercial, I want us to go to the pool. We can make fun of all the old people's bodies."

"Yeah, sure," Seth says, rubbing his arm. "Um, don't take this the wrong way, but is it cool if I don't watch you do your commercial? It's not that I don't want to, it's just I don't know how long that's going to take, and I haven't eaten anything."

"Oh, no, I don't mind," Bridgette says. "I honestly didn't think you were."

"Bridgette, I..."

"Relax. You're okay. Here." Bridgette takes a debit card out of her back pocket and hands it to Seth. "Whatever you want is on me. Try to mention you're part of the crew for the commercial, though." She winks. "You might be able to get something for free."

"Thanks," Seth says, taking the card. "Text me when you're done filming."

"Yep. See you soon!" Bridgette runs off.

Seth stands there, upset with himself for not asking Bridgette where to actually get food. He begins to wander the country club, passing running children and slow-walking adults of varying ages. Despite wearing essentially what every man is wearing, Seth still attracts a few odd looks, here and there. He eventually stumbles upon a bar. He takes a seat on a stool beside a girl around his age. She's talking to the bartender about something Seth can't make out.

"Excuse me," Seth says to the bartender, "you got any bourbon?"

The bartender nods. "You got any ID?"

"Never mind," Seth says.

"I tried, too," the girl says. Her hair is dyed a dark purple. "This guy is as stubborn as we are dry."

Seth turns to face the girl. "I wouldn't bother him, he's just doing his job. What's your name?"

"Melanie."

"Hey, Melanie, the name's Seth. Do you wanna keep me company while I go get some food?"

"Sure," Melanie says. She gets off her stool. "Beats hanging out here."

"Thank you," Seth says, getting up. He and Melanie walk outside where some workers are serving food off the grill.

"Why are you here, today?" Melanie asks, getting a hot dog.

"I'm here because of a friend. She's an actor, and she's doing a commercial about water or something."

"Your friend is a girl?"

"My friend is an actor, yes," Seth says.

"Are you dating her or...never mind. You would've said you were dating her. Are you gay?"

Seth laughs. "No, I'm not gay. I used to date her, but we broke up last year."

"Then why are you here?" Melanie asks again. The two begin to walk over to an enclosed area, plates full.

"I don't know. She called me this morning for the first time since we broke up and asked me to come with her." The two sit at a table.

"Don't you think that's weird?" Melanie asks. "Sounds like she still likes you."

"I'm sorry," Seth says, shaking his head. "You're asking me questions like you know me. What are *you* doing here?"

"I'm asking you questions because I don't *know* you," Melanie says. "But since you're being difficult, I'm here because my dad likes to golf here every Tuesday."

"Is that so," Seth says, taking a sip from a soda can.

"Yep, since I was twelve. He just lets me wander around

until six in the afternoon, and I meet him in the parking lot."

"That sucks."

"Not really," Melanie says. "I find ways to have fun." She leans in and whispers, "Do you wanna have fun?"

Seth leans in and whispers, with a smile, "It must be pretty cool if we're whispering."

Melanie giggles. "Ditch the food and follow me."

Seth nods and does as he's told. Melanie leads him to the back of a bathroom away from everyone else. She takes out a coin purse and shows it to Seth. He peers in, and his eyes light up.

"You have those sniffles about you," Melanie says, taking a dollar bill out of her other pocket. She rolls it up. "I figured it wasn't a cold." She goes to snort but stops. "Will your friend care?"

Seth takes a moment to shake his head. "No. You're sharing this with me?"

"Well, yeah, duh," Melanie says. "To help you ignore those old farts looking at you." She snorts up some of the cocaine and Seth follows suit. The two of them eventually sit on the ground, coin purse empty, and begin to kiss. About five minutes in, Seth's phone vibrates.

"Mm." Seth lightly pulls away from Melanie and looks at his phone. "Uh, Bridge...my friend is done with her commercial." He looks up at Melanie. "I gotta go." He hands Melanie his phone. "But, hey, give me your number, and I'll hit you up sometime. Promise."

Melanie smiles and begins typing on Seth's phone. "It's a date, funny guy." She hands Seth his phone back, and he makes his way to the pool.

"Oh, it went so well," Bridgette says. She and Seth are sitting in chaise lounges by the pool, both wearing shades and swimsuits. Bridgette looks at Seth. "I hope I didn't take too long."

Seth shakes his head. "Not at all. I kinda like this place. The food's nice."

"I'm glad you're having fun. Thank you again for coming. I wouldn't have felt right being here by myself."

Seth looks over to Bridgette. "Why did you ask me to come with you?"

"I've never done these things alone. Usually, my dad's here but..."

"No," Seth says. "Why did you ask *me*?"

Bridgette is silent. She looks away from Seth and says, "I guess I still miss you."

"Even though I was an asshole?"

"You were still my best friend."

"Then why didn't you talk to me?" Seth asks. "For a whole year, you didn't talk to me, Bee."

"I needed to grow up."

"You told Toby he needed to grow up. You needed to focus on yourself, and I see you've done that, and I'm happy you're happy. But I've been alone in that house with that freak taking over with no one to talk to, not really. I missed you, too."

"I'm sorry," Bridgette says. "To be honest, I was too embarrassed to ever come back. For the past year, I've been avoiding you and the guys. It isn't fair to any of you guys, especially you, and I'm sorry." Bridgette takes off her shades and begins to cry. Seth steps over to her, rubbing the tears from her cheeks.

"Maybe we should skip the fireworks tonight," Seth says. "We can go somewhere more private and spend some time talking about all of this."

Bridgette nods and puts her shades back on. "Can you drive me home? I walked here."

Seth nods, and the two of them gather their things. The drive to Bridgette's house was silent, but halfway through Bridgette takes Seth's right hand and holds it. When they make it to her house, Bridgette asks Seth to come inside until her dad comes home.

"When will he be back?"

"Tomorrow."

Seth and Bridgette go inside and to her room. The pair lie in bed for hours talking until the late evening. One moment, they looked into each other's eyes, put their hands on their cheeks, and the fireworks light up the sky.

13

TO BE KIND

That September, Bridgette knocks on Seth's door. She had called him the night before, but he didn't answer, let alone call back. She hadn't talked to Seth since July, but what she needed to tell him now was of great importance. She knocks on the door again, louder, and a few seconds later, Eric opens the door. He's yawning and wiping one of his eyes with the back of his hand.

"Good morning," Eric says. "It's nice seeing you."

Bridgette gives Eric a hug. "It's nice to see you, too," she says, then steps back. "I've heard some of your music."

"Yeah," Eric says, "whatcha think?"

"A little loud, but I like it, overall."

"Toby writes the lyrics, you know. He's not as good as his mom, but I think he gets the job done."

"Is Toby here?" Bridgette asks. "I mean, I'm here to see Seth, but it would...never mind. It might be too awkward."

"Well, luckily for you," Eric says, "Toby isn't here. At least, his car isn't." He peeks out the door. "Or Mom and Dad's. I guess it's just me and Seth."

Bridgette turns around and looks at the two cars in the driveway. "Which one is yours?"

"I'm sorry?"

"The cars," Bridgette says, turning back to Eric. "Which one is yours?"

"Oh, uh, neither. I don't have a car, I just get rides from whoever is here."

Bridgette raises an eyebrow. "If your parents are gone and Toby isn't here, then why are there two cars in the driveway?"

Eric becomes silent. After he notices his suspicious silence, he says, "I think Seth is still sleeping. Maybe you should come back later."

"It's 11 A.M., and I'm sure it's fine if I talk to him real quick. It's kinda urgent."

"Could I take a message?" Eric says.

"I think it's best that he hears it from me." Bridgette shakes her head. "What's wrong, Eric?"

"Now just isn't the best time to talk to Seth."

"Why? What's the matter?"

"I..."

Bridgette pushes past Eric and walks to the living room, looking around. The room is empty, and Bridgette starts toward the basement. Eric runs in front of her at the beginning of the hallway.

"Look, Bridgette, now isn't a good time."

"Let me through, Eric."

"Can we sit and talk? We haven't actually talked since last year. Seth told me that your commercials are going well."

Bridgette pushes past Eric again and makes her way to the basement door. She hears a woman giggling and puts her ear to the door to be sure. She hears what sounds like wet kisses and steps away from the door. She turns and walks back to Eric. "I think I'm gonna stay here for a bit."

Eric awkwardly goes into his room, and Bridgette goes back into the living room and sits on the couch in silence. About half an hour later, the basement door opens, and Bridgette hears Seth talking to someone else. He steps into the living room with Melanie close beside him. Seth stops in his tracks when he sees Bridgette looking back at them.

"Oh, hey," Seth says.

"Who're you?" Melanie asks, twirling her blue hair with her finger.

Seth extends his hand toward Bridgette. "Melanie, this is my friend—"

"Don't," Bridgette interrupts. She stands from the couch and faces Seth and Melanie. "I don't need you to speak for me."

"Okay."

Bridgette looks at Melanie and says, "I don't care who you are, but I need to talk to Seth."

Melanie notices Bridgette's blonde hair and says, "Wait, are you Bridgette?"

Bridgette looks at Seth. "You've told her about me?"

Before Seth can speak, Melanie says, "He told me you're his actor friend that does the commercials. It's been months, but I finally get to meet you!" Melanie walks toward Bridgette to shake her hand, but Bridgette steps back.

"What do you mean by 'months?'"

"Seth and I met at the Rivers Country Club. He said you invited him to support you for your commercial, but he ended up hanging out with me for a couple of hours."

Bridgette, shocked, looks from Melanie to Seth. "You were talking to her at the country club?"

"Bee," Seth says, "I can explain."

"What were you two doing in the basement?"

"I think I should go," Melanie says. She gives Seth a kiss on the cheek, followed by a 'Call me later,' and then walks out of the house.

Seth begins to walk to the kitchen, but Bridgette steps in front of him. "Just tell me," Bridgette says. "Are you fucking that girl?"

Seth stands there, looking at his feet. "Yes."

"For how long?"

"Since the day after the Fourth."

"Asshole." Bridgette walks toward the front door.

"Bee, I'm sorry."

Bridgette swiftly turns around, pointing her finger at Seth. "Don't you fucking call me that!" She takes a step toward him. "Did that night mean nothing to you? After you told me how much you cared about me and how you missed me too, you fuck me and tell me you don't want to have any kind of relationship with me?"

"Bridgette..."

"But this *entire* time, you've been fucking that blue-haired freak? What the hell is wrong with you? Seriously, what kind of shitty human being do you have to be to do that to someone?"

"I moved on from you, okay," Seth says. "I thought I missed you, but I guess it was just nostalgia or something. I don't know. I did enjoy talking to you, I did. After we had sex, though, I thought to myself that you weren't someone I needed in my life."

The two look at each other until Bridgette sighs and says, "I'm pregnant, Seth."

Seth does a double-take. "Seriously?"

"Yes. You are the only person I've ever slept with, so..."

"I, um, what do you want to do?"

Bridgette steps back. "Now I'm not sure *what* I want to do." She lightly bumps into the door, turns around, and opens it. "I'll call you. Please answer next time."

"O-okay."

Bridgette exits the house and walks back home. When she makes it, she bumps into her dad on his way out. "Hey, sweetheart," Mr. Miller says. "I was just about to get lunch. Do you want to come with me?"

"No, thank you," Bridgette says with a tiny smile.

"Okay," Mr. Miller says. He kisses Bridgette on the forehead. "I'll be back soon, then. I love you."

"I love you, too."

Mr. Miller goes out to his car and pulls away. Bridgette locks the door after him and grabs a chair from the kitchen as well as a boxcutter from a drawer of tools. She goes into the bathroom, closes the door, and puts the top of the chair under the doorknob. She turns on the cold water for the tub and sits in it, still clothed. She takes the blade out of the boxcutter and stares at herself in its reflection, a tear going down her cheek.

14

THE FAMILIAR TASTE OF
LONELINESS

A few hours later, Seth gets a call from Mr. Miller.

"Hello?"

"Hey, Seth," Mr. Miller says. He clearly sounds distressed.

"Hey, man, what's wrong?"

"The comedy club won't be open tonight. Or for the time being. I need to take some personal time off."

Seth sits up from the couch. "Is everything okay?"

Mr. Miller sighs, but it soon turns to crying. Seth silently listens to him cry from the other line. "Between you and me, Seth, because you two were close, it's Bridgette."

"What happened?"

"I...found her in the bathroom with her..." Mr. Miller stops speaking and begins to sob. After a while, he manages to say, "She tried to take her own life, Seth. I don't know what happened, but I need this time to focus on her. I'm sure you could run the place on your own, I just don't want to worry about any issues coming up. Do you understand?"

"Um, yeah," Seth says. "Where is she?"

"We're at the hospital. She's sleeping, so I stepped out to call you."

"Thank you for telling me."

"I'll talk to you later, Seth."

"Yeah."

Mr. Miller hangs up, and Seth stares at his phone. His hands begin to shake, and he quickly calls Melanie. He taps his foot on the floor for about half a minute before she answers.

"How'd the thing with Bridgette go?" Melanie asks. Seth can hear the distorted sound of her driving with the windows down.

"Oh, it was nothing. I'm...sorry if that made you awkward or anything."

"It was nothing, really. Are you sure you're okay?"

"Yeah," Seth says, then he pauses. "I mean, no. Do you want to come back here?"

Seth can hear Melanie's smile. "You wanna hang out or do something a little more fun?" she asks.

Seth stands up and paces. "Fun, I guess. I just really miss you is all."

"Maybe you should come to my place. Your parents should be home soon, and they might spoil everything. You don't want the night to be spoiled, do you?"

"No, I don't," Seth says. He looks out the window and sees it's getting dark out. "Oh, uh, I don't have work tonight."

"That's awesome! What happened?"

"Something came up with my boss. He said he had to take some personal time off and couldn't risk any issues coming up." Seth turns around and leans his back on the window. "Can I stay the night tonight? And maybe tomorrow?"

"You promise you won't get bored of me?"

"Of course, I won't get bored of you."

"Then meet me at my place. I'll be waiting."

"Do I park down the street or anything?" Seth asks.

"My dad's only here on Mondays and Tuesdays."

"That's awful."

"Just come over." Melanie makes a kiss sound to the phone and hangs up. Seth grabs his shoes by the door and puts them on. He then grabs his keys and walks over to Eric's room door, knocking.

"Are you gonna go talk to Bridgette?" Eric asks. "She sounded pretty upset earlier."

"Tell Mom and Dad that I'm gonna be here tomorrow."

"Where are you going?"

"Out. Um, Bridgette's not okay, so I won't be working tonight or tomorrow. But don't tell Mom and Dad that."

"I won't, but are you okay?"

"No, but I will be. I'll see you later, man." Seth turns to leave but says, "Hey, where's Toby, by the way?"

"I don't know. I think he's out trying to find someone to sign the band."

"He could just pay *them* instead."

"Shut up, man," Eric says.

"Just don't tell him anything either, okay?"

"Yeah, whatever."

Seth goes out and drives to Melanie's house, using the pin drop she sent him. By the time he gets there, it is pitch black outside except for the porch light. Seth rings the doorbell and hears Melanie run down the stairs and to the door. She opens it.

"I got us pizza!"

"You did?" Seth asks, stepping inside. The inside of Melanie's house was surprisingly plain to Seth, with pale wallpaper covering the walls and a few family photos here and there.

"I did," Melanie says, closing and locking the door. "I also bought some popcorn. I figured we could watch a scary movie or two..." She turns around, and Seth grabs her and pulls her to his lips. The two kiss for a few moments until Melanie gently pulls back. "If we're going to have fun, let's head to my room."

"With pleasure," Seth says, letting her go.

Melanie takes Seth by the hand and leads him upstairs to her room. They go inside, and Melanie locks the door behind them. The walls in her room are a pastel pink, and she has several stuffed animals scattered about. She pushes Seth onto her bed, then climbs on top of him, kissing him.

The two do this for a few minutes, then Melanie suddenly gets up. "Oh my god," she says. "I forgot to tell you I got us something." She walks over to her chest drawers and takes out a tiny plastic bag with two tabs in it. She faces Seth, who's still lying on his back, and smiles, jumping with excitement. "I was saving these for a special moment, but since you're going to be here for a day or two, I think now's perfect!"

Melanie climbs back on top of Seth, takes the tabs out of the bag, and tells Seth to open his mouth. He does so, and she puts a tab under his tongue, then proceeds to put the other under hers. "Good thing we didn't eat," she says. They cuddle until the tabs dissolve and begin to kiss again.

Seth doesn't remember too much after that. Melanie puts music on, at some point, and turns the room light off. She turns on LED lights, and they flicker to different colors as time goes on. Seth and Melanie embrace each other, switching from rabid to passion as they become closer. Seth sees stars on the ceiling, shining brighter as he tells Melanie stories about his childhood, and then becoming dimmer as he talks about his living situation with Toby.

Their sounds escape from their mouths out into the room and then back into nascent ears; the walls vibrate and breathe in tune with the beating of their hearts, without missing a beat; seated on the floor, they cry and laugh until they're bored; stomach churning from the taste of the material (or anything that isn't you); sucking face for the familiar taste of loneliness, shared with the always welcoming escape from hate, a warm embrace; lights are red, keys ignite, as souls race into welcoming dark; the stars are bright as the radio plays with her on top, hoping he doesn't come out of the dark; a moan that floats across all worlds; just you and her, as the radio plays and says with just one verse...

That hurts

How did I change my mind?

I swore you had a death-wish

How'd you think you get the head rush?

I loved the way you made me feel

It's all coming back to me...painted faces know their places

It's such a downfall

It hurts

"I'm glad you changed your mind."

"SETH, ARE YOU OKAY?"

Painful vomiting. Seth's throat burns as he's out on his front lawn on his knees, Eric crouched beside him. The alarm of Seth's car is blaring as the front of the vehicle is damaged from hitting the side of the house. The driver's door is wide open since Seth had to stumble out to safety before falling on the cool grass. At first, the only lights on the street were some neighbors' porch lights. Upon hearing the crash, Eric turned his on and other lights from inside houses were starting to come on.

"Dude, what happened?" Eric exclaims, his arm around Seth's back. Seth aggressively vomits again and falls face-first onto the grass. Eric screams, "Somebody help!"

The four corners of Seth's mind snap back into place, and soon after, his world turns black.

15

———

SOBER

Everyone is tired and itchy on Seth's first day of Narcotics Anonymous. After his incident on his front lawn, Eric informed Seth that he had been gone for three days. Seth didn't remember much from those days, but after going to sleep on the couch that night, Eric went online to search for nearby NA meetings. The closest one was an hour away from Rivers in Streamsville. Seth calmly agreed to go to the meetings when his parents and Eric confronted him. Toby sat in the corner of the room, his head down as he listened.

Seth and Eric's parents gave Seth the day to rest and also called Rivers High School to let them know of his situation.

After classes, Toby drives Seth to Streamsville for his meetings.

"I'll be out here in the car if you need anything," Toby says. Part of Seth believes he means it.

The NA meetings are shared in the same building as the Alcoholics Anonymous meetings, causing overlap between attendees. Many of the visitors ended up in the right place;

however, the NA crowd were visibly not happy with the alcoholics that willingly chose to be in the NA room. The building is considerably run down, being rented out for the sole purpose of these meetings. It has a stale smell that lingers on one's clothes.

"What is your name, son?" the group leader asks Seth.

"Seth."

"Hi, Seth," everyone says in unison.

"How do you feel about being here?" the group leader continues.

"I don't feel good, I'll tell you that much."

"Why is that?"

"This place feels...strange. It's scary and culty and...well, strange."

"Cults are just passionate people who are dedicated toward a cause," the group leader says. "In that regard, I guess we are indeed 'cults.'"

Seth covers his face with his hand. "Who the hell talks like that?"

"I'm sorry?"

Seth uncovers his face. "Nothing. Are you going to ask why I'm here?"

"I already know why you're here, Seth. You wish to be sober, and we're here to help you see that through."

The first day more or less continued like this. At the end of the meeting, the group leader assigned Seth a sponsor, a young woman named Abigail. Seth didn't care for Abigail, who always came off as aggressive.

"If you leave, you'll die!" Abigail had locked Seth in a room on his fourth day and had screamed at him for two hours. "You can't leave, you've barely even started. You're already getting more color in your face. You don't understand that if you leave there're only three outcomes, and they're all downhill."

Seth, sitting in a wooden chair in the corner of the room, looks up at Abigail. "What three outcomes?"

Abigail crouches down to Seth's eye level and says, "Jails, institutions, or death. We're here to help you. Your family asked you to come here to get help, and you're not even brave enough to give it a try."

"I did give it a try. Four fucking days, to be exact. I'm done. I don't want anymore." Seth looks down at his shoes, but Abigail puts a finger under his chin and makes him look at her.

"You're such a failure. You're a goddamn comedian, you're sixteen, you're in NA, and you won't even accept help to become rehabilitated."

Seth pushes Abigail's hand away. "That's what I'm talking about! All you guys have done since I've been here is harassed and guilt-tripped everyone."

"We don't do anything of the sort," Abigail says.

Seth stands from the chair. "You do, though. Whenever someone new like me talks about their experience, someone that's been here longer will compare their trauma. As if having a shittier life is cool. It's like having a less shitty life is frowned upon here." He sits on the floor in the middle of the room. "I understand that I need help. I don't really remember what happened when I took that acid, but I was not *there*"—he gestures to his head—"for three days. I just don't understand how I'm expected to continue on the right path when you've been screaming at me. Besides, I don't even see why the fuck it matters. I finally had a bad experience, so I'm not going to *do* anything again."

Abigail, still equated, hobbles over to Seth. "That's the

thing, Seth. There are Not-Yets. Sure, you'll leave here and won't do cocaine. Not yet, at least. You won't do acid, then you'll decide that's no fun, so you'll try heroin. Not yet. It never ends until you decide you want to be sober."

"I'm deciding now!"

"No," Abigail exclaims. "You're deciding to run away from your problems again. Your friend Bridgette tried to commit suicide, and you think it's your fault. So, you ran to your girlfriend and went on a three-day drug binge. You have the power to look your fear in the face and tackle it head-on. You just have to look it in the face first."

"Just let me out of this room. This is illegal."

Abigail leans closer to Seth. "If you don't promise to see these ninety days through, I'll let the authorities of Rivers know that your little girlfriend Melanie has something illegal in her room."

"What the fuck?"

"We know who you are, and we know *far* more powerful people than you, including some people you associate yourself with. So, do the right thing and make yourself a better fucking person."

Seth stares at Abigail, frightened. He swallows and says, "It's just for ninety days?"

Abigail nods. "After that, you can do whatever the hell you want. Quitting any time before then will be a grave mistake."

"Who are you people?"

"See the program through and you won't have to know."

"So, I've been going to Narcotics Anonymous meetings for the past three weeks. First of all, I didn't even know that NA was a thing. My brother came up to me the morning after I crashed my car into my house and said 'I signed you up for NA', and I asked him 'Why would you sign me up for something that's not available."

The audience laughs.

"So, we're having our meeting, and our group leader announces that he bought everyone pizza. There's gonna be sixteen pizzas coming in just a few minutes. So, everyone is as excited as tired and itchy addicts can be for pizza. By the way, doesn't anyone else find the concept of putting other addicts in the same room as each other weird?"

The audience laughs.

"It's like these guys came together and asked themselves, 'Hmm, there's a growing number of people, particularly youth, who are struggling with substance abuse. Now I know that religion is slowly going out of style and herd mentality is definitely a thing, but what can we do, without science, to help those in need?' They wait there for a moment and 'GASPS! I have the perfect idea, Jim!'"

The audience laughs.

"This pizza party, this fucking pizza party. Some people were actually cheering when they saw it come in. And our group leader didn't skimp. Pepperoni, sausage, cheese... hell, just fucking pineapple if you wanted it. He ordered a shit ton of sauces, too. You know, the typical stuff: garlic, marinara, ranch, that type of stuff. And my sponsor, I won't say her name, asks me to get her pizza for her. 'Sure, why not?' I go up to the table and grab us both a plate and come back to sit by her. 'Oh,' she says, 'can you get me some napkins?' I get up and I go get her some napkins. I come back and sit and she says, 'Can you get me an extra plate? I'm scared that the grease will make this one too flimsy.' I get back up, go to the table, and grab another plate. I come back to sit by my sponsor, and she asks me to get her some ranch cups."

The audience laughs.

"And I. Fucking. Flip. I scream at her that I'm not a server and this isn't a restaurant. I use this annoying voice and say stuff like 'Can you get me another glass of water? Can you get me an extra fork? Can you get me an appetizer? I know my entree is in front of me, but I really want an appetizer.' And everyone is staring at me, by this point. I say to my sponsor, 'I'll get you your ranch cup, but you have to remember that other people exist. I could've gotten all of that at once and would've been fine. Instead, you had me go back and forth. What the fuck is wrong with you?' I finish screaming at her, and it's quiet for a while. Then I started crying."

The audience laughs.

"I'm crying the hardest I've ever cried in my life at this stupid pizza party at a NA meeting. I caused a whole scene when all these other people are just trying to eat pizza and go home or whatever. I became fully aware that these other people exist."

The audience laughs.

Seth clears his throat. "I guess what I'm trying to say is don't do drugs. You'll find yourself screaming at your NA sponsor about ranch cups. Thank you." The audience of the comedy club cheers, and Seth walks off stage. He walks outside to Toby's car, who lets him borrow it to go to work, and fumbles to get the key out.

"Nice set, tonight."

Seth turns around and sees Richard standing with his black leather jacket and jeans on. Seth unlocks the car door and begins to get in. Richard steps toward him.

"Woah, now, take it easy," Richard says, grabbing the car

door. He closes it before Seth can get in. "I'm not here to cause any trouble. I wanted to say that it's good to see you, kid."

"The feeling isn't mutual."

Richard raises his hands, amused. "Harsh words, kid." He lowers his hands but points his thumb toward the building. "Are you really in Narcotics Anonymous?"

Seth nods.

Richard whistles. "Wow. You know, I can't help but feel I'm responsible."

"You are responsible."

Richard waves his finger. "No, sir. I gave you some coke over the summer, sure. But, I remember giving that rich kid some when he first moved here, and I don't see him wildin' out. It sounds like you lack discipline."

Seth gets in Richard's face. "You gave minors drugs and alcohol, and you're trying to give me a lesson?" He pushes Richard. "You almost ruined my life, you bastard."

"No, kid. *You* almost ruined your life. I did the same stuff when I was your age, and you don't see me needing to go to meetings. It's you, kid. Face it."

Richard reaches into his jacket and takes out a brown bag shaped like a bottle. He waves it a little. "I got you something. As a welcome back gift." He hands the bottle to Seth. "If I'm really at fault then you'll learn from your mistakes and not drink that. Or at least in moderation." He turns around and begins to walk back to the comedy club. "Catch you around, kid."

Seth sits in the car, looking at the bottle long and hard. He takes the top off and takes a sip. He puts the bottle down and raises it back to his lips, taking several gulps. He spends the next hour sitting in the car, drunk, laughing, and crying to himself. Someone opens the back door of the comedy club.

The audience laughs.

16

TREMOR CHRIST

On Halloween night, A Taste of Tongue held a special concert in Streamsville inside a building by the lake. Toby had made it to where the start of the concert was right after Seth's NA meeting so Seth could attend. Of course, Seth didn't have much choice since Toby was his ride. Halloween was on a school night, so the theme was to have A Taste of Tongue play until past midnight and for the show to be exceptional for the attendees or their money back. The show started at 8 PM, so the band would have to play for four hours, which had Chris and Eric worried as they didn't have enough original material to do so. Toby, however, had stated that whenever the band ran out of material then he could sing covers alone on stage.

Fans began arriving early, around 6:30 or so. Chris and Eric were eating dinner from a nearby fast-food restaurant while Toby waited outside of the NA building for Seth. Chris and Eric talked to the fans, who told them that they appreciate what A Taste of Tongue has done for the community. Chris and Eric did not know what the fans meant by this, but they appreciated the sentiment.

When Toby arrives around 7:55, he swerves into the parking lot. Some fans see this and cheer when he and Seth step out of the car. Toby walks through the crowd, into the building, and heads for the stage, leaving Seth.

"Are you ready to rock, Streamsville?" Toby says on the microphone, fixing his hair. The crowd cheers, and Toby says, "Thank you all for coming out tonight, especially on a work and school night. But don't worry, we promise to make it all worth it in the end. One, two, three, go!"

The band begins to play, and Seth stands in the crowd of raving strangers. He never expected the band to even get remotely big, so being here and seeing Toby's recent success makes Seth feel small because of what he saw as failures. The band plays on and on, with Seth standing with his lonesomeness until he spots Bridgette about thirty feet away. She is nodding her head out of tune to the music and is tapping her foot, her hands in her jacket pockets, as usual.

At first, Seth's heart skips a beat. He hasn't spoken to Bridgette since she told him she was pregnant. She doesn't look much different now. Her stomach is bigger, for sure, but it isn't as huge as he expected it would be. Seth suddenly feels his mouth becoming dry, and he begins to feel a little hot. He knows, though, that he needs to talk to Bridgette, to check on her and see what they can do about her pregnancy. Seth begins to make his way through the crowd and taps Bridgette on the shoulder. She looks at Seth with a face that if she could frown some more she would.

"Hey," Bridgette says, just loud enough for Seth to hear. In a building as loud as this, it would be normal to scream, but Bridgette cannot spare the energy.

"Hey," Seth yells, an appropriate volume given their location. "I wanted to talk to you. If that's okay?"

"Of course you do."

"I think it's important that we talk to each other, you know," Seth says. He points his thumb behind him and leans closer to Bridgette. "Do you wanna get out of here?"

Bridgette nods, and the two of them go through the crowd and out the door. The cool air is a shock, and Bridgette immediately hugs herself as Seth puts his hands in his jacket pockets. They face each other.

"So," Bridgette says, "what is it you want to talk about?"

"I guess the first thing I want to know is how you've been?"

"I've been better."

"But you've also been worse."

"Yeah," Bridgette says. "I imagine my dad told you what happened. As if everyone in Rivers didn't find out soon after."

"Word gets around fast, doesn't it?"

"You didn't visit me," Bridgette says, shivering.

"I know. I had something come up with me, as well."

"So I've heard. Are you okay, man?"

"I..." Seth starts. He looks around and gestures with his head for Bridgette to follow him. They start walking toward the water. "I relapsed last week. I drank a whole bottle in the car and cried."

"You haven't done anything else, though? Since then."

Seth shakes his head. "No. I haven't done any drugs since I started about a month ago."

"That's great. I'm proud of you."

"Thanks."

They come across a fishing boat with the key still in it.

Seth gives Bridgette a look, and she shakes her head. "No way," she says. "We'll get in trouble."

"They're all distracted by the show." Seth steps inside the boat. "Come on, it'll be fun. And private."

Bridgette hesitates, but then says, "What the hell," and steps inside the boat. She sits in the passenger seat, and Seth sits and turns the boat on. He drives the boat across the water until they can't hear the concert. Seth then turns the boat off, and he and Bridgette sit in silence, with only the sound of the water surrounding them.

"It was wrong what I did to you," Seth says. "With the whole Melanie situation. I lied to you and said I didn't want any kind of relationship, and I realize that I hurt you. I've hurt a few people, but no one as much as you."

"Do you still talk to her?"

"I haven't talked to Melanie since my incident with the acid. I don't know if she reached out to me or not. I blocked her the morning after all that happened." Seth pauses. "I sometimes think about shooting her a text and seeing what she's up to. I know that wouldn't be wise, though."

"Do you think she would've supported you? At NA."

Seth looks at the stars in the sky. "I think so, actually. She's a little bratty and clearly has a couple problems, but I think she cares about me. It's weird."

"Yeah."

Seth turns to Bridgette. "What's even weirder is that we're gonna have a kid."

"Yeah."

"Unless you don't want to. I mean, we're still young, so I understand. Or maybe you wouldn't want a kid by me."

Bridgette sighs. "It's nothing like that, Seth." She looks down at her shoes. "I was pissed at you when I learned about Melanie. And even though you were part of it, you're not the only reason why I tried to kill myself that day." She looks away so Seth can't see her face. "I'm not...happy. And I don't know why. I mean, I know why because my mom wasn't happy, so I got it honest. I've always been unhappy, and no matter how many successful commercials I do, how many wonderful people I meet, or how much I laugh, it doesn't get easier. It *hasn't* gotten easier." She looks at Seth. "I hate you for how you took my feelings and shit on them, but I still care about you. I'm happy you're getting better at NA, and in a weird way, I hope you talk to Melanie again. But, I don't think we should have a baby. Not when I'm broken."

"Oh." Seth grabs his shoulder and looks away.

Bridgette gets up, goes to the edge of the boat, and gets on her knees. Looking at her reflection, she says, "Do you think my mom went to Hell for killing herself?"

"You know I don't believe in that type of stuff, Bee."

"Bee...that would've been a good name for a girl."

"Maybe, yeah," Seth says. "Who knows, though, right?"

"Yeah, who knows," Bridgette says, her watch locket in her hand.

The sound of the water comforts them.

"I think," Seth says, "to answer your question, if there is a God and there's Heaven and Hell, then your mom would be okay. I mean, she was depressed. Wouldn't that be God's fault? He made her that way, just like he made you that way. It's messed up that he made you guys that way, but suicide isn't a form of failure, I feel. I don't know about religion, really, and I'm rambling, but if God made your mom depressed, and He made you depressed, then surely people like you get a free pass. Your mom's in Heaven looking down on you and is proud of you for what you've accomplished and how far you've come. I don't think any good person goes to Hell."

A splash.

Seth turns around quickly and sees that Bridgette isn't on the boat anymore. He quickly gets up and runs to the edge of the boat. He sees Bridgette's watch locket on the floor, open to the picture of her and her mom.

"Bridgette!" Seth screams. He takes his shirt off and dives into the water after her.

17

A LITTLE EXTRA FOR THE TRAUMA

Seth comes back up on the fishing boat with Bridgette. He puts her on the floor of the boat, then gets on his knees. Bridgette is still conscious and is crying. Seth gets her on her knees, wraps his shirt around her, and hugs her.

"It's okay," he says, comforting Bridgette. "It's okay, I'm here."

"But for how long?" Bridgette cries. "How long before you leave me again? Everyone's going to leave me." She cries harder, and Seth holds her in silence. Seth lets Bridgette cry for a few minutes until she seems to calm down.

"I have an idea for what will make you feel better," Seth says. "I've been going to the NA meetings for the past month, and they've really helped me out. Maybe you can go with me?"

"I'm not on drugs, though," Bridgette says softly.

"No, but I think they can help you by listening to their talks. It might soothe your soul."

"Do I need my dad's permission to go?"

"No. In fact, the next time I go you can come with me,

and I'll get you settled. Toby drives me there, so you can ride with us, if you're okay with that?"

"That's fine," Bridgette says. "Thank you, Seth."

They hug for a while longer, then Seth pilots the fishing boat back to shore. They get in the backseat of Toby's car after Seth cranks the car and turns the heat on. As the concert plays on, they both eventually fall asleep. They both awake with a jolt when Toby opens the driver's door.

"Hey, you two," Toby says, halfway in the car. He notices Seth's shirt is off. "Am I interrupting?"

Seth yawns and stretches a little. "No. She just fell in the water and needed to warm up, that's all."

"Ah," Toby says, sitting in the car and closing the door. He puts Chris's guitar in the passenger seat. "How'd you get here, Bridgette? I mean, do you need a ride home?"

Bridgette unwraps Seth's shirt off her and puts it in Seth's lap. "My dad let me borrow his car tonight. I can drive home."

"You sure?" Toby asks, looking at Bridgette via the rearview mirror.

"Yeah. Thank you." She looks at Seth and says, "Thank you, too. I have the same number, so text or call me whenever you get the chance."

"Of course," Seth says quietly.

Bridgette gets out of the car and waves goodbye to Toby and Seth. Toby turns to look at Seth in the backseat. "Are you okay, man?"

"She's gonna be riding with us to go to my NA meetings."

"Is she…"

"No. She's just feeling a little lost. Where are Eric and Chris?"

"They found some girls to hang out with or something. The girls said they'll drive them home tomorrow."

"Yikes," Seth says with a yawn.

Toby turns around. "You wanna stay in the backseat or come up here?"

Seth lays across the back of the car. "I'm gonna sleep here."

THE NEXT MORNING, there's a knock on Nowell and Brianne's front door. There's no answer, at first, so another knock follows. A few moments later, Nowell opens the door.

"What the hell are you doing here?" Nowell exclaims.

"You didn't think I'd eventually come knocking on your door," Janie says. "I remember when you would always knock on mine."

Nowell steps outside and closes the door lightly.

"Brianne home?" Janie asks.

"Yes, she's in the shower. Now answer my question, what the hell are you doing here?"

"You and your wife announced a new album about a month ago. The great big comeback album, marred by controversy."

"What of it?"

Janie laughs to herself. "'What of it?' The entire reason you stopped making music was that you wanted to raise your son. He may be a teenager, but he's still got some raising to do."

"Toby is quite successful for his age, and Brianne and I believe that all the groundwork for him is done."

"You seriously believe that?"

"I do," Nowell says.

"Well, I hope your little comeback album is a one-off because I think you've gotten a little too comfortable, Nowell."

"Just say it, woman."

"Remember the last time we talked?" Janie tiptoes closer to Nowell and whispers, "When you and I kept each other up all night?"

"What of it?"

"What was the one thing I asked you to do for me?"

"I don't remember, what?"

Janie brings her mouth close to Nowell's ear. "To give me another chance," she whispers. She backs away, smiling.

Nowell stares at her, shocked. "What the fuck are you saying?"

"You have another son, Nowell. Eight months old. Oh, you should've called. It would have made this a whole lot easier."

"You're lying."

"Am I?" Janie takes out her cell phone and shows Nowell pictures of their son. "Isn't he adorable?"

"What do you want from me?"

Janie puts her phone away. "I already told you, another chance. I need money, Nowell. You've tried to escape me for over twenty years, and I almost let you get away with it. But you know how this world is now, and money is hard to come by. I came to you last year asking for your help and you said no. You called my bluff when I told you I would tell your little secrets, but now I'm serious. Give me enough cash to raise our son on my own, or divorce your wife and do it with me. Last time you did *it* with me made me think your wife isn't enough for you."

"Shut up."

"It's never enough for you, Nowell. You had a family, and you gave it up for fame. You had your fame and you won't let it go, not even paying your dues to me."

"Does she know?"

"Of course, she doesn't know," Janie says. "I kept my word, and now it's time for you to keep yours. I'll give you some time to make your decision. I know where you live, so I'll come to you. I hope you make the right decision."

Janie walks off, and Nowell stands on his front porch, breathing heavily.

"CHRISSY!"

There's a loud knocking on Chris's screen door. Chris is in his room sleeping after being dropped off around noon by a girl he met last night. He opens his eyes upon hearing the knocking, and his head feels like it got hit by a truck. He leans up in his bed and groans. The knocking on the screen door continues, and Chris gets out of bed, leaves his room, and opens the door. It's almost dark out, and he sees his uncle standing outside with a trash bag beside him.

"Good afternoon, rockstar," Richard says. "How was school today?"

"I didn't go."

"Little rockstar Chrissy playing hooky. With a hooker, too."

"What the fuck do you want, Richard?"

"I need you to do your uncle a favor."

"Why would I ever help you do anything?" Chris asks, rubbing his forehead.

"You're a feisty little prick today, aren't you," Richard says. "Listen, it's nothing really. My car's in the shop, and I need to take out some trash. I just need a ride to the dumpsters on the way out of Rivers, that's all."

"Why can't you get Aunt Becky or your stupid girlfriend to take you?"

"Because your aunt is out of town, and Sheila isn't feeling well."

"Bullshit."

"Hey, if you don't believe me," Richard says, raising his hands, "then come over to my house and see for yourself." He puts his hands down. "Come on, I'll make it worth your while. I'll give you fifty bucks now and another fifty when we make it back. 100 bucks for twenty minutes of your time." He takes out his wallet from his back pocket and hands Chris two $20s and a $10 bill. What do you say?"

Chris sighs. "Okay, fine. Give me a sec."

"Thank you, Chrissy," Richard says, smiling wide.

Chris goes back inside the house to put his shoes on, grabs his keys, and heads back outside. He unlocks the car door and pops the trunk. He gets in the car while Richard puts his trash bag in. Richard then gets in the passenger seat. "The dumpsters on the Streamsville Highway?" Chris asks.

"Yes, sir," Richard says.

"Okay."

Chris pulls out of his driveway and drives to the Streamsville Highway. He turns the radio up loud to avoid talking to Richard. Chris feels awkward the whole ride since Richard seems content with not talking. After about ten minutes of driving, Chris makes it to the dumpsters. There's a singular black truck in the gravel lot, and Chris parks away from it.

"No, no, no, Chrissy," Richard says, waving his hand. "Park closer to that guy."

"Why? We have so much space here."

"Just do it."

Chris parks beside the black truck, and a man steps out.

Chris pops the trunk, and Richard steps out of the car. Richard nods at the man.

"Sorry if I took too long," Richard says. "My car's in the shop, so I had to bum a ride from my nephew."

"Ain't nothing but a thing," the man says. "You got the shit?"

"Yeah, right here." Richard reaches into his jacket and takes out a big plastic bag of cocaine.

"What the fuck?" Chris says quietly to himself in the car.

The man hands Richard a wad of cash and takes the cocaine from him. "Pleasure doing business."

"Pleasure's mine," Richard says. He gets in the passenger seat and begins counting the money as the man gets into his truck.

"What the fuck was that?" Chris exclaims.

"That was making an honest living," Richard says. "You could learn a thing or two if you hang out with me. Maybe you'll learn how people less fortunate than you survive on a daily basis."

"You're scum, you know that, right?"

"No, I'll tell you who's scum," Richard says, pulling a handgun out from inside his jacket.

Chris raises his hands. "Woah, woah, take it easy!"

"That piece of shit in the truck, right here! He fucking shorted me!" Richard quickly gets out of the car, leaving the door open. He taps his gun on the driver's window of the truck and then shoots the man in the head through the glass.

"Holy shit!" Chris screams.

Richard then puts the gun back in his jacket and takes some gloves out of one of his back pockets. He puts the gloves on and reaches into the truck to unlock the door.

After opening the door, he takes the bag of cocaine back and stuffs it in his jacket. He gets back into the car with Chris.

"Come on, Chrissy, let's go back home."

Chris, shaking, begins to pull away before Richard starts shouting, "Wait, wait, wait!"

Chris stops the car, and Richard gets out and runs to the trunk. He takes the trash bag out, closes the trunk, and throws the bag into the dumpster. He gets back in the car. "Okay, let's go home. I almost forgot."

Chris pulls out of the gravel lot. "What the fuck just happened?!"

Richard, taking his gloves off, says, "I know, right? The dumb motherfucker thought he could gip me? No, sir, not in my city. I would've spit on that piece of shit, too, if it weren't for the few good cops here." Richard looks at Chris. "Thank you, Chrissy. I'm sorry you had to see that. But, let that be a lesson to never be deceitful. You can have your whole life ruined by lying. With that being said, don't tell anyone what happened, okay?"

Richard reaches into his back pocket and takes his wallet out. He gets out a $100 bill and puts it in the cupholder. "Here, a little extra for the trauma. Before you drop me off, stop by the ice cream shop when we first make it to town. I have a hankering for shaved ice that I can't get my mind off. I'll get you something, too, Chrissy. On me. The sundaes are to die for."

18

PRETTY DONE

"You okay, Chris?"

Chris jumps out of his haze. Backstage before a show, Toby asks again if Chris is okay as he seems distant.

"Yeah, I'm fine. Just a little nervous."

Toby pats him on the back. "Well, don't be. Word is that there are a few label execs lurking around in the crowd. We gotta be on our A-game."

"I'll be fine once we're out there."

"Good," Toby says. "Tonight might be our big break." He walks off to go get a bottle of water.

Chris sits in a chair, waiting for the show to start. It's been three days since he saw his uncle shoot the man at the dumpsters. Chris hasn't been sleeping well since the incident, and the loudness of the concert-goers outside has been keeping him on edge. He sighs and puts his face in his hands. Eric walks up to him.

"Scary, right?"

Chris looks at him. "What is?"

Eric gestures toward the crowd. "Someone out there

might change our lives forever. All we have to do is play our dicks off."

"Terrifying."

"You think we're up to this?"

"We'll see when it's over," Chris says.

"I guess so. It's never really over, though."

"What?"

Toby comes back with a half-empty bottle of water. "Alright, you guys ready?"

Eric flips his bass around, and Chris stands up, grabbing his guitar. They both nod.

"It's showtime."

The group goes on stage, and the crowd cheers.

"Hello, Rivers!" Toby yells into the microphone. The crowd screams louder. "Are you ready for the best night of your life?" More cheers. "Well, without further ado, I'm Toby Lewis-Green, and these other two gentlemen are Chris and Eric. We're here to give you a taste of tongue. One, two, three, four!"

The show was hands down A Taste of Tongue's best-ever performance. Toby had spent time reworking his lyrics, and although they were still not great, they were greatly improved. His vocal performance was also notice-ably different, with all the words being spat, slurred, or mumbled. Chris was on top form despite still being distracted by what happened a few days prior with his uncle. He chose to take his feelings out through the music, and he even did a couple guitar solos—something that Toby stated he did not want in the band. Eric chugged along on his bass and added flair to his solo openings that made the crowd applaud. After a forty-five-minute set, everyone involved experienced what could only be viewed as an overall good show.

After the show, the bandmates hung out behind the building, talking to fans and signing autographs.

After a while, Elisha walks up to Toby.

"That was a great show you played tonight, boys," Elisha says. "Better than your Halloween one, even."

Toby nods. "Thank you. We appreciate you coming out to see us." He turns to Chris and Eric. "Aren't we, guys?"

Chris and Eric nod and reply, "Thanks for the support, man."

Elisha smiles. "Absolutely. We have to support the Rivers community in any way we can. Young people like you guys are doing *fascinating* things in the art world, here in Rivers."

Toby, looking back at Elisha, says, "Thank you so much for your kind words."

Elisha leans in. "Now, Toby, you're the son of Nowell and Brianne from Lonely Souls, correct?"

"That's me, alright. They saw I was doing my own thing, and I guess now they want to make another album."

"That interview they had was awful," Eric says.

"Sure was," Chris says.

"But we don't try to put any focus on where I came from," Toby says. "People were naturally curious about us in the beginning because of who my parents are. But I think those that stay are definitely still here because we make awesome music, and Lonely Souls being my parents is just a nice little fun fact, when it's all said and done."

"Well, Toby, I hope this isn't too awkward for you," Elisha says, "but what if I told you A Taste of Tongue and Lonely Souls might soon be labelmates?"

"Why's that? You know someone?" Toby steps closer to Elisha. "I've been talking to people online about trying to get a record deal, and some of them said they'll be here tonight. You heard someone out there talking?"

Elisha chuckles. "No, I used to be in Lonely Souls for a little while back in the 90s. Before your parents even got married." He hands Toby a business card, and Chris and Eric huddle around. "I'm also the founder of the label they've been signed to for all these years. My name is Elisha." He reaches out his hand. Toby gathers himself and shakes it. "I'm a very good friend of your parents."

Elisha shakes Chris and Eric's hands and continues, "I've been watching you boys for some time, now, and I've made the decision that I want to sign you guys to a record deal."

"Oh my God," Chris says.

"You have my business card," Elisha says. "Stop by my home on North Treadwater Street tomorrow so we can talk. I think we can all come to an agreement. What do you say?"

Toby looks at Chris and Eric. "What do you guys think?"

"We should definitely talk tomorrow," Eric says. "But I'm predicting we'll reach an agreement."

"Chris," Toby says.

"Hell yeah, man, we'll talk to him!"

Toby looks back at Elisha. "It's a date."

Elisha smiles. "Awesome. Well, any time you guys are ready tomorrow just stop by. I'll be home all day." He then walks off, waving. "I look forward to speaking with the three of you."

When Elisha is out of eyesight, the three boys jump up and down, cheering. They all hug and high-five each other.

"I told you guys that we could do this," Toby exclaims. "This time tomorrow we're gonna be legit!"

That night, after dropping Chris off and going home, Toby calls Nowell. The phone rings for a while, but Nowell eventually answers. Toby responds, stuttering initially since he hasn't spoken to his father in over a year.

"Hey, Dad."

"Where are you?" Nowell asks. "Is there anyone around you?"

Toby is standing on the front porch of Seth and Eric's house, shivering in the cold. "Not really, no. I'm at home—"

"Where do you live? Go outside. If you're already outside, walk far enough away that no one can hear you."

"Okay," Toby says, confused. He walks off the porch and about thirty feet away from the house. "I think I'm good now."

"What the hell do you think you're doing calling me? Your mother told you not to contact us unless you made a name for yourself."

"I have, Dad. My band's been going pretty well."

"So I've heard. But, some people think you're a plant."

"Well, what did you expect?"

"Don't blame me," Nowell says. "Your mother is the one who kicked you out."

"You've supported it all this time, so you're equally to blame." Toby sighs. "I was calling you because tomorrow my bandmates and I are probably going to get signed."

"Congratulations," Nowell says, coldly. "Who are you signing with?"

"That's the thing," Toby says as he walks down the street. "We talked to this guy named Elisha. He told us he's known you and Mom since the beginning of Lonely Souls."

"Dark-skinned man, slender?"

"Yeah," Toby says. "He said you guys are signed to him, and he wants to sign my band."

"Interesting."

"I initially wanted to call you to say that we'll probably be labelmates soon, but now I'm thinking is this even a good idea."

"What do you mean?" Nowell asks.

"Is this a trap or anything? He wants us to visit him at his house tomorrow. I don't know, but Mom told me that she could have me killed, if she wanted to, and I don't understand why we'd go to his house."

"Why would your mother have you killed?"

"So, she *could* get me killed?"

"Listen, Toby," Nowell says, "Elisha's record label is based in the United Kingdom. He's the founder, and he talks to acts here in America, but he's not the president of the label, and he lives here in Rivers."

Toby stops in the middle of the road. "For how long?"

"A while now."

"Is that why we moved here? It wasn't random or anything like that?"

"Toby, go to Elisha's house tomorrow and talk to him about your band. If he's interested in signing you then he's genuinely interested. It's not because you're...who you are."

"I think it is because of who I am, Dad."

"Just talk to the guy if you want to live a happy life. Better than the one your mother and I gave you, at least."

"Will Mom be upset about this?" Toby asks, walking back to the house. "About us technically being co-workers?"

"I'll make it clear that it's all a coincidence. I gotta go, Toby."

"Okay, Dad. Bye."

Nowell, having already hung up, is sitting in a chair in the corner of his room. Brianne is in the bathroom, just now getting out of the shower. After drying off and getting dressed, she comes into the bedroom. Nowell gets up.

"What's the matter?" Brianne asks.

"Okay, I'm gonna make this quick. Remember when we crashed our yacht last year and that woman saved us?"

"Yes."

"Well, Bri, she came to our house recently and spoke with me. She told me that when I was sleeping back then, she came into the room and took some of my sperm, and now she has a baby with me."

Brianne gasps and covers her mouth. "Oh my God."

Nowell begins pacing the room. "She said that if we don't give her any money then she'll go to the media and say I raped her and told her to keep the whole affair a secret. But I got one thing better for her." He takes Brianne by the hands, and he has them both sit on the bed. "We go to the media and announce that I cheated on you, and I have an illegitimate son."

"Do you think anyone will believe that?"

"Half of the world already thinks that anyways. We'll say that the initial rumors last year weren't true, and the pressure of trying to maintain a healthy family life amongst the rumors caused me to turn to alcohol. I slipped up not too long after we moved to Rivers and had a one-night stand with the woman."

"This is terrible, Nowell! I wish these women would leave us alone."

"It'll be okay, Bri. Because what we'll also do is pay this woman what she asks for and also take in the baby as our own."

"What?"

"It's like before. When Toby was about to be born, we had one more album to make. But, we gave it up to be a family. Now we've made that album, Toby's moved on, but we are given another chance to be a family again. We'll paint it as if *Vestigial* is about this drama we've been living through and we've made it through it."

"Are we actually raising that woman's baby?"

"What other choice do we have," Nowell says. "This *may*

be a legitimate way for us to restart. Another chance to make our mark on the world."

"What if it fails?" Brianne asks. "What if they hate us just like they did after our interview?"

"They didn't hate us, Bri. They were just skeptical. But, once we announce to the world that this baby exists, they'll rethink the interview and see that it all makes sense." He brings Brianne's hand closer to him. "We *will* be remembered."

19

———

TREADWATER

The next day, around noon, Toby, Chris, and Eric met with Elisha at his home to talk about the band's future. Upon arriving, Elisha made tea in the kitchen, while the boys sat on the couch in the living room. When the tea is finished, Elisha comes into the room with four teacups on a big plate. He has the boys each take a cup of tea and he lays the plate on the table between the two couches.

"Okay," Elisha says, sitting on the couch across from the boys. "Sorry that it took so long." He takes a sip of tea. "Let's get right to it. My plan for you guys is quite simple. I want us to have a two-year contract, one studio album required." He points to some papers on the table. "I have all of that in there. I will provide you with full creative control. The only things hindering you will be the time, which is of course two years, and relocation."

"Where will we be relocated?" Toby asks.

"We have a recording studio in Canada that I think will suit you guys nicely. We'll need to get passports for you, however, so in the meantime, you'll be writing material here and recording demos, if any, on your own time."

"How will we be getting to Canada?" Eric asks. "And what do we do after one album?"

"You will be driven out to Canada. We don't really fly unless it's an emergency or overseas. After you complete your album, you'll be going on tour to support said album. You must begin your tour in England, that's where our headquarters is located. Anything past that is up to you. Again, we like to give you plenty of freedom. We do prefer that you communicate to us in advance when you'd like to perform, and that way we can properly schedule when the time comes."

"So, after one album and a tour we're free to go?"

"If you so choose after two years," Elisha says. "Once we're close to that two-year mark, I'll talk to you guys again and see where your headspace is. If you're still interested in working with us, then we'll do another, more long-term contract. We like for new artists to get their feet wet first. How are we feeling?"

"I mean, yeah," Chris says. "But, what about school? We're still teenagers."

"We hire professional home-schoolers who teach you what you need to know until you graduate. Education is all provided for, and we're very strict about it, so you *will* learn. Any more questions?"

"I don't think so," Toby says.

"Okay," Elisha says. "Now, I can have the three of you sign this contract, but it wouldn't actually mean anything without getting permission from your guardians. On the top of that stack of papers are consent letters. If you guys are on board, I need you to take those papers and bring them to your guardians. Have them read the fine print, and if *they're* on board, have them sign the consent letters. Bring the papers back to me, and I'll have you guys sign the rest. Once you guys are 18, you will sign a letter confirming that you understand our recording agreement, just now as an adult."

"Sounds good to me," Toby says. He looks at Chris and Eric. "Boys?"

"Sounds great," Chris says.

"I always wanted to go to Canada," Eric says.

"Perfect," Elisha says. He grabs the papers off the table and reaches them over so Toby can grab them. "Take these to your guardians, and once they sign bring them back to me. We can then start working on getting you guys passports."

"Thank you," Toby says.

The four of them stand and shake hands. "Again, you have my business card. Just call me if you need anything. Otherwise, I'll see you when I see you." The boys exit Elisha's home.

"So," Eric says, "how do you want to do this? I was thinking we can get all our parents to meet somewhere, and that way we can all see this stuff together."

"That's a good idea," Toby says. "I'll go over to my parents' house and ask them if we can all do it there. I figure my parents will know how to read a contract."

"Great," Chris says. "You take the papers then. I think I'm gonna head out. Catch a movie or something." Chris begins to walk toward his car. "I'll see you guys later."

Toby and Eric wave at him, saying, "See ya." They walk to Toby's car and get in, and he cranks the car.

"When are you gonna talk to your parents?" Eric asks.

"As soon as I drop you off," Toby says. "It's hard to believe this is happening."

"I know. By the end of the year, hell, maybe even by the

end of the month, we'll be out of Rivers."

"We won't get trapped here."

"You were never gonna be trapped here," Eric says. "You can move whenever you want. Chris and me? Our lives are gonna take a huge trajectory."

Toby glances back and forth between Eric and the road. "Thank you for believing in me, man. It was you and Chris that started this band. You guys asking me to join gave me a goal, and we just achieved the first of many."

"Of course," Eric says. "It was really nothing. We just thought that you were already talented because of your parents. And Seth was no help."

"This city's changed my life. I'm gonna miss it when we leave."

"We can always schedule a show here whenever that album comes out," Eric says. "Hey, do you think your parents moved here because they knew Elisha lived here?"

Toby shakes his head. "I don't know. I asked my dad yesterday, but he kinda avoided the question. I'm beginning to think so.

Eric's phone vibrates, and he looks at it. "Holy crap."

"What?" Toby asks.

"Um, dude, your mom and dad just announced that they have a fucking baby."

"What?"

"No, dude, this is crazy. They went to Mayor Waterston's to make an explanation video or something. Your dad said he cheated on your mom sometime last year, and now he has an eight-month-old son." Eric reads on. "And they said they're taking in the kid to raise him and that their new album is about what they've been dealing with since moving to Rivers. Dude, what the actual fuck is wrong with your parents?"

"Do you think that's what that rumor was last year?" Toby asks. "That my dad has been cheating on my mom?"

Eric looks over at Toby. "You're joking, right?"

"About what?"

"About not knowing what the big rumor was last year?"

"No," Toby says. "They didn't tell me, and I just never bothered to look it up."

"Why not? Look it up, I mean."

"They're my mom and dad. I care about them."

"Well," Eric says, "If you never looked it up and your parents didn't want you to know, I guess I'll only tell you a little bit."

"A little bit?"

"It's slightly more complex than you think it is," Eric says. "It's just that...it's not too surprising that your dad cheated on your mom."

"That doesn't tell me much of anything."

"At this rate," Eric says, "I think the day will come when it will. Your parents are slowly turning into a nightmare."

Toby didn't say anything in return as he didn't want to talk on the matter anymore. Meanwhile, Elisha also received the news notification that Nowell had a new son. Elisha had turned the television on to check the news station to see the big announcement, but he missed it. He takes his phone back out and goes to his contacts to call Nowell. The phone rings until Elisha is told to leave a voicemail.

"Hey, Nowell, call me when you get a chance. I saw on my phone you and Brianne's big announcement. Congratulations, of course, but also you guys did not discuss this with me before telling the whole world. Please call me back, when you get a chance, and remember that we *all* have a reputation to keep. Bye."

Click.

20

LIE, CHEAT, STEAL

Toby dropped Eric off at home, then drove to Nowell and Brianne's house. At first, Toby was nervous since he hadn't been to the house in over a year. Outside of the house, Toby takes deep breaths in his car before he gets out. He walks up to the front door and rings the doorbell, the papers from Elisha in his hand. Brianne answers the door.

"It's you," Brianne says, coldly.

"Hi, Mom."

Brianne looks at the papers in Toby's hand. "I imagine one of those is a consent letter?"

Toby nods. "Yeah, this is everything actually. My bandmates and I were wondering if we could come here to read all the paperwork. Like, their parents come here, as well."

Brianne gestures to the papers. "May I?"

Toby nods and hands the paperwork to her. Brianne flips through most of the paper, then says, "I'll be right back." She goes inside with the paperwork and closes the door. Toby stands outside awkwardly until Brianne comes back.

"I had your father sign his share, and I signed mine, as well. Do you know the names of your bandmates' parents?"

"No," Toby says. "Look, I wanted us all to read this stuff together to make sure we're all on the same page."

"Toby," Brianne says, "trust me when I say that they'll be on the same page as me and your father." She hands him the paperwork. "Now please leave my goddamn house."

Brianne goes inside and closes the door. Toby stands there, shocked at first, then he sighs and walks back to his car. He drives to Chris's house and has Chris's parents sign the consent letter. Toby then goes home and has Seth and Eric's parents sign their part.

"So, what now?" Seth asks Toby in the kitchen after dinner. "You guys are just gonna move to Canada?"

"After we get our passports, yeah. I don't really know how long that takes."

"Congratulations, man." Seth pats Toby on the back and begins to wash dishes. "I didn't think the whole band thing would go anywhere, but I'm really proud of you."

Toby turns in his chair to face Seth. "Are you gonna be okay while Eric and I are gone? For NA."

"Yeah, I'll be fine. I mean, I might need to get a new car soon, but having Bridgette there will make things easier. Thanks for asking."

"You know," Toby says, "Since I'm leaving, I could lend you some money for a car."

Seth shakes his head. "Thanks, but I think I'll be okay."

"You sure? I can get you a used car since you'll need something to drive to Streamsville."

Seth looks at Toby. "Seriously, man, it's okay."

"Alright," Toby says. "I, uh, just wanted to do something specifically for *you*." He looks at the ground. "I came in and took over your life, and you've gotten nothing in return." He looks back up at Seth. "What's the least I could do?"

Seth stops doing the dishes and sighs. "Bridgette's pregnant, man."

"Really?"

"Yes, really. I don't know what to do. *She* doesn't know what to do. She said she doesn't want a kid because she doesn't want another generation of unhappiness, but I think it'll be good for her. Good for *us*." He looks at Toby from the sink. "She tried to drown herself at the Halloween show. She needs a break. Toby, the least you could do is find a way to make her happy, for all of us."

"I think financial security will help," Toby says. "Maybe my parents will take you guys in."

Seth scoffs.

"No, I'm serious," Toby says. "My parents are gonna start raising their baby and they really want and need good publicity. If you show up at their door and ask them for help, they might actually do it."

"You seriously think so?"

"It's worth a shot."

Seth knocks on the counter. "Okay. I think I'll try that tomorrow. Worst case is they say no." Seth walks out of the kitchen and into the hallway. "Goodnight, Toby."

"Goodnight, Seth."

The next morning, Seth walked to Nowell and Brianne's house to ask for help. He knocks on their door and whistles nervously, thinking Toby's advice will not work. Nowell and Brianne both answer the door and look at Seth, confused.

Seth laughs awkwardly. "Um, hi." He waves his hand a little. "You guys don't know me, but I'm a friend of Toby. I have a proposition for you guys."

"Make it quick, kid," Nowell says.

"Right," Seth says. He gathers his composure. "So, I saw on the news yesterday that you guys have a baby now. Well, I have a baby on the way, and I'm really excited about that. But I'm also nervous because, um..." Seth pauses for a bit, then says after sighing, "Look, Toby has been living with me and my family since last year. I don't know if he ran out or you guys kicked him out, but you guys need good publicity."

"We already have good publicity," Brianne says, taking her designer shades off.

"Yes," Seth says, "But more is always better. You guys are raising a baby together that isn't even yours, ma'am, no offense. That's part of your whole story—you stopped making music to raise a child. But now you're making music as a direct response to having a child."

"What are you getting at, kid?" Nowell asks.

"My girlfriend, our baby, and I can be your goodwill. Look, my girlfriend and I are also in NA—"

"Not helping your case," Nowell interrupts.

"But it does. Think about it: 'Nowell and Brianne from Lonely Souls raise an illegitimate child while also taking in two NA members and *their* child. You guys will be seen as heroes."

Nowell and Brianne look at each other for a few moments, then to Seth. "How much do you want from us?" Brianne asks.

"All I ask is for financial security to raise my kid."

Nowell crosses his arms. "You have a deal *if* you go to an actual rehabilitation center instead of NA. Also, if you help raise our baby as well as yours."

Seth nods. "Then it's a deal."

Brianne steps inside, and Nowell takes a step forward. He extends his hand, and Seth shakes it. "Very well," Nowell says. "You and your girlfriend can move in whenever you want. Just let us know in advance, so we can announce it." Nowell gives Seth his phone number and goes inside the house. Seth begins to walk back home, calling Bridgette to tell her the good news.

Around that time, Toby, Chris, and Eric gather at Elisha's house again to sign their contract. The four of them are in the living room again, and Elisha has just finished making sure all the papers are signed.

"Excellent," he says, clapping his hands together. "Now that all the paperwork is complete, I can get your passports. In the meantime, you boys can start writing songs here in Rivers and even play a few shows before you have to go." He stands, and the boys follow suit. They all shake hands before Elisha says, "I promise you, this is the beginning of the best days of your lives."

21

SILENT SINGLES

A year and a half later, Toby, Chris, and Eric successfully finished recording their first album. The move to Canada was rough for them as their passports came around Thanksgiving of 2017. They first arrived in the winter, so they spent most of their time indoors. Originally, the bandmates thought this was a blessing in disguise since being inside more surely meant more time to write. But, the three boys were miserable and homesick and didn't come up with much material. By springtime, dissatisfied by the lack of results, Toby made Chris and Eric promise to fully complete a song each month.

"It's March now," Toby said. "If we just focus on doing one song each month, then we can have around eighteen or so songs by the end of next year. Worst-case scenario, we would have a small tour that lasts about a month or so before our contract ends."

Chris and Eric agreed since the plan was better than nothing. Fifteen songs later, Toby calls Elisha to inform him that the long-awaited album is finally completed.

"Perfect," Elisha says. "I'll start making plans for you guys to head over to England and start playing some shows. Remember that if you want to go anywhere specific to let me know. Because of how long it took you guys to actually record your album, we're gonna try to shoot for a release next month. But, we have to figure out which one of these songs is a lead single so that we can build hype."

"I know you just said our album should be out in a month," Toby says, "But when should we expect to be leaving for England?"

"Don't know yet," Elisha says. "It could be tomorrow, it could be two weeks from now. You guys just sit tight and relax. Congratulations on making it this far." Elisha hangs up, and Toby tells Chris and Eric the news.

"We should definitely go to Rivers," Chris says. "I think it'll be good for the press, plus we get to go back home."

"You don't think that they'll think we're sellouts?" Eric asks. "We did sign a contract then up and leave on short notice."

"They're human," Toby says. "If they haven't already forgotten, then they'll forgive us once they see us play. How do you guys feel about England?"

"Eh," Chris says.

"I hear the summer is nice there," Eric says. "It could be fun hanging out there for a while, actually. I don't miss the heat in Rivers."

"I don't really miss Rivers, honestly," Toby says. "The people are nice here, and it's not as hot. Less drama, too."

"There wasn't that much drama until your parents showed up," Eric says, pointing. "I'm surprised that the place wasn't destroyed after their last album did so well."

"It's only a matter of time before they tear it apart," Toby says. "Trust me."

. . .

S ETH IS PLAYING with his son in the living room of Nowell and Brianne's house. He quit his job at the comedy club, believing that the late nights and, to a greater extent, Richard were pressuring him to relapse. Upon leaving, Nowell and Brianne had Seth enter a 90-day program at the Rivers Rehabilitation Center. Seth found his time there to be fairly easy-going, especially compared to Narcotics Anonymous, which Bridgette still attended.

As promised, Nowell and Brianne provide complete financial security to Seth, and he hasn't worked since leaving the comedy club. He has been a full-time dad to both his 13-month-old son and Nowell and Janie's 26-month-old son. Seth jumped headfirst into being a dad and frequently thanked Nowell and Brianne for their kindness.

"You did us a favor with my first son," Nowell said one night during dinner. "I guess it was only right that we help you with yours."

Seth finds raising Nowell's baby to be noticeably more difficult than his own. Now a full-grown toddler, he often whines and rarely eats anything remotely new or dairy. Nowell and Brianne haven't spent much time at the house since the release of *Vestigial*, so Seth can't ask for help. When they are at home, Nowell and Brianne remind Seth of their deal from 2017.

Today, Nowell is walking through the living room on his phone. He tries to avoid tripping over any toys. "He made one album, so what? Didn't you tell me they spent three months just doing nothing?"

"That's not the point," Elisha says on the other side. "I wanted to let you know that they'll soon be touring in England. I was wondering if that will be okay?"

Nowell makes it to the front door. "Yeah, it should be fine. I think at this point there's nothing to really worry about—"

Janie is standing at the front door, her fist in the air since she was about to knock. "Hello, again, Nowell."

Nowell quickly closes the door. "I'll call you back."

"Wait, what's wrong?"

Click.

"Who were you on the phone with?" Janie asks.

Nowell grabs her by the throat and walks her down the steps. He lets her go. "What the fuck are you doing here?" he says in a whisper.

Janie rubs her throat and clears it. "Aren't you a charmer? I came to check on our baby boy."

"*My* baby boy," Nowell says, pointing at himself. "We made a deal, Janie. You leave me and my family alone, and I finally do my time."

"Rumor is you aren't doing your time. You have some kid watching our boy for you. You know... since you and your wife are busy."

"You see the news, Janie. Bri and I are doing that boy a favor. All three of those boys."

"Look, Nowell, I'm just gonna cut right to it. I want my baby back. You spent most of the past year playing shows, staying in the media, and whatnot. You can't honestly believe that I, or anyone, seriously think that you've been taking care of our child."

"I don't understand how you could want *more* from me," Nowell says, his voice rising. He takes a step closer to Janie. "I gave you money, I took our child into a wealthy household, and I gave you the ability to do whatever the *fuck* you want. Yet, you want more."

"I just want you to take accountability," Janie says.

"Fucking accountability," Nowell says, his voice cracking. "For the past three years, you have literally been knocking on my door for me to take accountability. Now I'm doing it, so get out of my goddamn face, you blood-sucking bitch."

Janie slaps Nowell and points at him. "Don't you dare talk to me like that, you piece of shit! You know goddamn well what I want from you, and you still won't go to the public and say it."

"Leave her out of this," Nowell exclaims. "She's successful on her own. You'll ruin her."

"No," Janie says. "You're afraid of your reputation being ruined by someone other than yourself. I *know* you, Nowell and—"

"There you go saying you know me," Nowell interrupts. "You *knew* me. A shittier, younger version of me that has changed. And you can't accept that simple fact: that I've changed and you haven't. If you go to the media and tell the world, nothing good will come from it. Just leave Annalisa out of this, and let's all live our lives."

Janie stares Nowell down. "When was the last time you said her name?"

"It doesn't matter. Now please leave my house. I'm tired of fighting."

"This isn't the last you've heard from me," Janie says. She walks to her car and gets in, driving off. Not long after she pulls out of the driveway, she takes out a flip phone and dials a number. The phones ring for a bit, then there's an answer.

"How'd he take it?" Elisha says.

"About as well as you'd expect," Janie replies. She sighs. "Look, it's been three years, and he said he's tired of fighting. I'm tired of playing nice."

"So, what do you want to do?"

"What's the name of that teenager he took in, again? Seth or something?"

"Yes," Elisha says.

"I imagine he wouldn't listen to Richard if he came knocking on their door."

"I would assume no."

"Maybe we can still work with that," Janie says. "Who's the mom for that kid he's got?"

"A girl named Bridgette Miller. She still goes to the NA meetings. Nowell said that Seth asked if they could pay for a psychiatrist for her, but Nowell said no one would believe that sob story."

"We're gonna have to start with her," Janie says, awkwardly taking a cigarette out. "Start with her, then go to Seth, and then we can get to Nowell and Brianne."

"Alright."

"When's Toby getting to England?"

"Soon," Elisha says. "Sooner now after hearing about Nowell."

Janie exhales. "Okay. Have him there within the week. And try to take care of Bridgette by the end of the week, too. Everything should snowball from there."

"Of course," Elisha says. "I'm gonna call Abigail, now."

Click.

22

———

GLAZED OVER

The next day, Bridgette walks into the NA building in Streamsville. She nods and greets everyone as she makes her way to the back where the meetings are held. Before she can make it to the back, she's stopped by Abigail.

"Hey, Bridgette," Abigail says.

"Hey. What's up?"

"I was wondering if you could do me a favor, after tonight's meeting."

Bridgette puts her hands in her back pockets. "Whatcha got for me?"

"Well, I know you live in Rivers, and I was wondering if you can check on my uncle there."

"You have an uncle in Rivers?" Bridgette asks. "I didn't know that."

"I don't really like to talk about him," Abigail says, lowering her voice. "He was very abusive growing up, but he's still family, you know? Plus, it's hard to stay angry with someone who has dementia."

"I guess."

"Anyway, he hasn't been answering anyone's calls recently, and no one besides me lives close enough to visit him. I would check on him myself, but I have to stay home and babysit tonight. Can you please check on him?"

"Sure," Bridgette says. She crosses her arms. "So, uh, do I knock on his door or what?"

Abigail reaches into her pocket and hands Bridgette a key. "Here. This is one of his spare keys. Just go to 106 Robins Street and knock on his door. If he doesn't answer, use that key to go in."

"What if he's, you know, dead?"

"Then I apologize for traumatizing you," Abigail says.

"Fair enough."

Abigail gives Bridgette a hug and says, "Thank you so much! I owe you for this."

They let go of each other, and Bridgette says, "No prob. Just any time tonight?"

Abigail nods. "Yep. Please text or call me whenever you check on him, okay?"

"Gotcha."

After the meeting, Bridgette drives straight to 106 Robins Street in Rivers. She parks her car in the empty driveway and notices that this is the same street Chris used to live on. Bridgette gets out of the car and goes up to the front door. The outside of the house looks well-kept enough, and Bridgette tries to look through the windows, but the blinds are closed. The lights inside are clearly off, and the house seems to be empty.

Bridgette knocks on the door and stands for a few moments. No one answers the door, and there is not even a peep from inside. She knocks again, this time louder and firmer, hoping to have a more distinctive knock this time.

Still no answer. Bridgette sighs and takes out the key to unlock the door.

The key doesn't work. Bridgette tries jiggling the key while it's inside the lock and also tries shaking the door, but the lock will not turn.

"Fuck," Bridgette says, putting the key back in her pocket. She walks back down the few steps that lead to the front door and calls Abigail on her phone. Abigail doesn't answer, and Bridgette puts her hand in her pockets out of frustration. She decides to walk around to the back of the house to see if there's a back door. She makes it to the back and sees that there is indeed a door. There's also a window at the back of the house and Bridgette can see that there is a tiny lamp inside. Bridgette takes the key out again and inserts it into the lock. She turns the key, and the door unlocks with a satisfying click.

"Yes," Bridgette exclaims to herself before letting herself in. She closes the door behind her and puts the key into her pocket. "Hello," she says. "Abigail's uncle? I'm a friend of hers, and she asked me to drop by and check on you."

She walks through the hallway that connects to the back door and goes to the kitchen. In the kitchen, a lamp is on, and Bridgette starts observing the room. The kitchen isn't dirty, but there isn't a noticeable amount of food on display. Bridgette calls out again as she walks around the kitchen and stops in her tracks and gasps when she sees what's on the refrigerator.

On the refrigerator door is a picture of Chris when he was younger with Richard. Bridgette then remembers that Richard lives on the same street as Chris's parents and begins to turn around, only to face Richard standing in the doorway, a handgun pointed at her.

"Well, howdy," Richard says. "How do you like the place?"

"Hey," Bridgette says. "I'm a friend of Chris, but I'm not here to...I think I'm in the wrong house."

Richard takes a singular step forward. "You're not, Bridgette. In fact, you're in the perfect spot."

"How do you know who I am?"

"The folks at Narcotics Anonymous told me, that's who. We know a lot, such as Nowell and Brianne wouldn't let you go to an actual psychiatrist. Instead, they forced you to attend our meetings."

"Did Seth tell you that right before he went to rehab or something?"

"Someone told me," Richard says. "But it wasn't Seth. Do you really trust Nowell and Brianne with your baby?"

"Everything's fine up until now."

Richard laughs. "They're scum, you know that right? Well, Nowell's scum."

"What do you want from me?"

"I don't want anything," Richard says. "Some people hired me to get rid of you so they can achieve certain things."

"You have a hit on me!" Bridgette exclaims. "What did I do? I didn't do anything. Why would there be a hit on me? I just—"

Richard fires his gun and shoots Bridgette in the head twice. Her back hits the front of the refrigerator, and her body falls to the ground. The sound of the gun firing in the kitchen is ear-piercing, and Richard walks over to Bridgette's body. He takes some gloves out of his pockets and crouches down, searching Bridgette until he finds the key Abigail gave to her. Richard puts the key in his back pocket, stands up, and leaves the house through the back door. Leaving the door unlocked, the sound of dogs barking fills the air as Richard walks away from the house. He takes out a flip phone and dials a number.

"It's done," he says. "You can proceed to the next move." He snaps the phone in half and takes out his personal phone to call the police.

Seeing the news the next morning stunned Seth. He sat in the kitchen chair and stared at the tiny television, motionless. Nowell and Brianne come into the room and turn off the television. They sit in the other two chairs, and Brianne puts her hand on one of Seth's.

"We are so sorry for your loss," Brianne says. "I know it's soon, but Nowell and I need to go on TV to address what happened last night. We need you to contact Bridgette's father, so we can begin planning for her funeral, as well."

Seth sits silently.

Nowell leans in. "Is that going to be okay, Seth?"

"Yeah," Seth says. "Just take the kids with you, please. It'll look good for the press."

Brianne squeezes Seth's hand tighter. "You know we can't do that, Seth." She kisses Seth on the forehead, and she and Nowell get up.

"If anything comes up," Nowell says, "call us."

"We'll try to hurry," Brianne says.

After they leave, Seth turns the television back on and stares at the screen. What felt like mere minutes later, he sees Nowell and Brianne on stage in front of the Rivers Police Department. They talk about what happened last night as an absolute tragedy and that they are mourning as much as Seth, the father of Bridgette Miller's child. They go on to state that, although violence is lower than it was when they first arrived, crime in Rivers is still a part of everyday life in the city, and it must be stopped before more innocent lives are lost.

The rest of what Nowell and Brianne say is lost by Seth since his eyes glazed over because of his own sadness. Just like that, he has become a single father raising not only his but also the baby of two egomaniacs. Most importantly, though, Seth has lost his best friend.

23

———

SEED

In 2016, Nowell starts to put the tight women's clothes back on, while Janie begins to smoke a cigarette. "Don't," he says, "she'll smell it on me."

Janie sighs and puts the cigarette out in an ashtray on her bedside table. "Fine," she says. She flips over on her side and faces Nowell. "Stay a little while longer. I don't think she's waking up anytime soon." Janie brushes Nowell's back, and he stops.

"Okay," he says, taking the shirt off. He lays on his side, and he and Janie look into each other's eyes. They don't talk for a while until Janie asks a question.

"Are you happy, Nowell?"

"Absolutely."

"Not at this moment," Janie says. "With your entire being, are you happy?"

"I'm a successful musician, husband, and father. Of course, I'm happy. Why do you ask? Are you happy?"

"Of course, I'm not," Janie says. "How can anyone remotely intelligent be happy?"

Nowell chuckles. "What, only dumb people can experience happiness?"

"I think so, yes. Maybe not dumb but ignorant." Janie breaks eye contact. "Have you ever looked into a baby's eyes when they're smiling or laughing, and you just *see* that they are genuinely happy? They're not tainted yet by the cruelty of the experience we call life. No death, no taxes, no loans, and no disappointment. So many disappointments. None of that is there, and you can see it in their eyes." She makes eye contact again. "I can see in your eyes that you're unhappy, Nowell."

"What in my eyes say that I'm unhappy?"

"I don't know...there's still life in them, but it's like a footprint in cement, a relic of the past, of better times."

"Presumably," Nowell says.

"Maybe so. But I can tell you're tired, Nowell. Tired of living the life of the person you've become and not the person that you want to be."

"Fancy telling me who I want to be?"

"You and I both know who you want to be," Janie says.

Nowell looks away from Janie, deciding to reside in his thoughts. She continues to look at him, admiring him physically and longing for him before biting her lip and continuing to speak.

"I know you don't want to be with me," she says. "And that's fine. How long are you going to fool yourself that the timeline you chose is the right one for you, Nowell? It's sad to see what is and to be reminded of what could've been. You escaped Paleview physically, but your heart has always been there. You *long* to go back to your home."

"I have a home," Nowell says, "and it's not Paleview."

"It may not be, but there is an element of it that is, and

you know it. What will it take for you to make the decision that will make your life worth it?"

After only a few moments, Nowell says, "To hold the love that I felt when I was younger in my hands again."

Toby, Chris, and Eric are now preparing to head to the airport to fly to England. The boys pack as much as they can, even though they've been assured by Elisha that packing everything is unnecessary. While finishing up his packing, Toby gets a video call on his phone from an unknown number. He answers the phone and sees a young woman with short black hair.

"Um, hello," Toby says, plugging up earbuds to his phone. He puts them in. "Can I help you?"

"Hi," the woman exclaims. "Am I speaking to Toby?"

"Yes, you are."

"Awesome! My name is Annalisa Smith, and I'm the CEO of Svelte Records. It's nice to finally meet you, even though it's over video."

"Oh, hi," Toby says. "It's nice to meet you, too."

"Elisha informed me that you and your other bandmates are getting ready to board a plane to head to England soon, correct?"

"Yeah, we're packing now. It's supposed to be about a seven-hour trip."

"Right," Annalisa says. "Tomorrow, after you guys get some rest, you all will be meeting me, where we'll discuss marketing plans for your new album. Do you have a name for your album yet?"

"We do not, no."

"Well, we'll discuss that tomorrow, as well. Are there any questions you'd like to ask me to tide you over?"

"If you don't mind me asking," Toby says, "how come you're CEO and not Elisha?"

"I don't mind, and that's a great question. Elisha founded the label back in the 90s, not too long before I was born. He would travel back and forth from here to The States to recruit talent and help take care of me. By the time I was a teen, I showed an interest in business, and Elisha permanently relocated to Rivers while I became CEO and stayed here."

"Go back a bit," Toby says. "You said Elisha took care of you?"

"He didn't tell you? He's my father. I know it may seem as if it's nepotism, but I did genuinely work for my position."

"So, did you meet my parents before you became CEO?"

"I've actually never met your parents," Annalisa says. "Elisha exclusively works with them."

"Why's that?"

"He just always has. But enough chit-chat. I'll speak with you again tomorrow. Enjoy your flight!" She then hangs up.

Toby takes his earbuds out and begins to finish packing again, his conversation with Annalisa stuck in his mind.

THE DOORBELL to Nowell and Brianne's house rings, and Seth opens the door. At the door is Elisha, holding a bouquet of white lilies and a card.

"Hey there, Seth," Elisha says. "My name is Elisha. You might have heard of me."

"Here and there."

"Mind if I come in for a bit?"

Seth opens the door farther and steps to the side so Elisha can come in. Seth closes the door. Elisha thanks him and hands over the lilies and card.

"I heard about what happened and wanted to send my condolences," Elisha says. "It's awful to go that young and in such a violent way, too."

"I appreciate the kindness, sir, but can we please not talk about it?"

"Oh, of course. Sorry."

Seth sighs. "It's okay. Thank you for being the only person who truly seems to care. Nowell and Brianne left as soon as they heard so they could talk about the shithole that is this city." Seth sits the lilies and card on an end table. "It's good to know that people like you still exist out there."

Elisha smiles a light smile. "I only brought flowers and a card. It's the least I can do."

Seth shakes his head. "Several people have done less." He sits on a couch. "Is there anything else you wanted?"

"Oh, no," Elisha says, "but it does sound like you need some rest, Seth."

Seth rubs his eyes with his palms. "I know, I know." He looks around the room. "It's just hard."

"Losing a loved one is difficult," Elisha says, "but we all learn to keep fighting. Whatever it takes to get over the grief, we as people endure it until it's moved on to someplace else."

"How do you move on?" Seth asks. "Whenever you lose someone?"

Elisha shifts around a bit. "To be honest," he starts, then chuckles, "I just get high."

Seth laughs. "Really?"

Elisha laughs with Seth and says, "Yeah, seriously. I go home after a long day of work or grieving, and I just snort up."

"Snort up?"

Elisha smacks his head with his palm. "Oh, shit! I shouldn't have told you that. I'm sorry, Seth."

Seth waves his hand. "No, it's fine." He clears his throat. "So, um, I know this is a weird question to ask, but do you have any on you?"

"Any what?"

"You know," Seth says. "I just want enough so I can make it through today and maybe tomorrow."

Elisha stands in the center of the room, contemplating his move. "You're an addict, though, Seth."

"That was mostly for alcohol, even though it was NA. Look, man, I promise I'll do good."

Elisha reaches into his front pocket and takes out a small bag of cocaine. He cautiously hands it over to Seth, and they walk toward the door.

"Thank you," Seth says.

"Tell Nowell and Brianne I stopped by."

Seth nods and unlocks the door. Elisha tells Seth to take it easy and closes the door behind him. Elisha hears the lock click as he walks toward his car. He has the faintest smile on his face.

24

NOTHING

After locking the door, Seth stands still and listens to himself breathe. His heart is racing as he knows he shouldn't do what he's about to do. Seth looks at the tiny bag of cocaine in his hand, flipping it around as he delays the inevitable. He puts the bag in his pocket, turns around, and heads upstairs. He goes into what used to be Toby's room and checks on the two boys, who are sound asleep. Seth grabs his wallet off the dresser in the room and takes out a $1 bill. He puts the wallet back down and leaves the bedroom, closing the door behind him.

Seth goes into the hallway bathroom and closes the door behind him. He opens the bag and pours all the cocaine onto the kitchen sink. He then rolls the $1 bill, puts the tip into his nose, and proceeds to snort some of the cocaine. Immediately after doing it, Seth is washed over with a sense of euphoria he's never felt in his life. He puts the toilet lid down and sits on it after putting the $1 bill on the kitchen sink. He feels safe and warm as if he's meeting up with an old friend.

This is the happiest Seth has ever been—as well as the

calmest. He lays on his back on the bathroom floor and looks at the ceiling, rubbing his chest with his palm. He gazes at the ceiling and smiles until he goes to sleep.

Two hours later, Brianne comes home to get her checkbook. She opens the front door to the house and hears the two children crying upstairs. Brianne runs upstairs and sees Nowell's son sitting over Seth's body. The young boy looks at Brianne as she comes in and gasps, tears running down his eyes.

"Seth," Brianne exclaims. She goes over to Seth and leans down, putting two fingers on his neck to search for a pulse. Nothing. Brianne then shakes Seth's body and still nothing happens. Tears start to swell up in Brianne's eyes, and she puts her ear to Seth's chest. She leaves it there for a few seconds, then quickly brings herself back up, gasping. Nothing.

Brianne takes the child's hand and goes out of the bathroom into the bedroom with Seth's crying son. She picks him up and carries him, the three of them going downstairs and to Brianne's car.

"Shh, it's okay, babies," Brianne repeats to the children. "It's okay." Brianne buckles both children into car seats and then proceeds to get in the driver's seat. She takes out her cell phone and calls Nowell.

"What is it, Bri?" Nowell answers.

"Nowell," Brianne says, her voice cracking. "Seth is lying on the bathroom floor, and he's not moving." Brianne deliberately chooses not to use the word 'dead' in front of the kids. "I felt him and listened to him and nothing."

"Okay, okay. Just come back to me with the kids. We're gonna have to do another speech."

Brianne cranks the car. "I'm on my way with the kids now. Start the speech without me. Speak from the heart."

"I always do," Nowell says.

Brianne hangs up the phone and pulls away. Nowell puts his phone in his pocket and sighs. He's inside the Rivers Police Station after making a speech about Bridgette's death. With a glass bottle of root beer in one hand, Nowell rubs his forehead with the other. His phone rings, and he fumbles it out of his pocket before answering.

"Hey," Elisha says from the other line. "I'm outside the police department. Can you come out back to see me?"

"Yeah," Nowell says. "Of course. Just give me a few." He hangs the phone up and walks outside the police department. After walking around to the back, occasionally taking sips of his root beer, Nowell sees Elisha. The two approach each other and start talking.

"Now's not the best time, Elisha," Nowell says. "Brianne just called me and told me that Seth's dead."

"I know he is," Elisha says.

Nowell takes a step back. "What do you mean by that?"

"I came over to your house and gave him some coke laced with fentanyl."

"You fucking what?" Nowell screams.

"Be quiet," Elisha whispers, shushing Nowell. "Let me explain myself, okay? Look, I've been talking with Janie."

"So it *was* you," Nowell exclaims. "I've been wondering how she got here and how she found me. Why the fuck have you been talking to her?"

"Nowell, she and I think there's a way we can all be happy. We gave you an out, just now."

"By killing that innocent young man?! He had a kid! *My* kid was there!"

"I know, I know," Elisha says, stepping toward Nowell. Nowell takes another step back, shaking his head. "I'm sorry for that, for *all* of this. Janie and I are giving you the opportunity to reveal your past, and everyone can be happy."

"How can I trust you when you've been talking to that bitch?" Nowell screams. "And for how long, Elisha? I want everyone to be happy, too, but this feels wrong."

"I know this feels wrong," Elisha says, "but I promise that we're doing what needs to be done." He reaches his hand out to comfort Nowell, but Nowell slaps it away.

"You and that woman are about to ruin my life," Nowell says. "How can you do this to me, after all we've been through? I thought you were my friend?"

"Nowell," Elisha says calmly, "I am your friend. Just lower your voice and we can talk—"

"Fuck you!" Nowell exclaims. He takes the root beer bottle and smashes it across Elisha's face.

"Ow, fuck!"

Elisha falls to the ground, on his knees and grabbing his face. A couple of moments later, three police officers come around the corner of the building. They see Elisha on the ground, his face bleeding, and Nowell standing over him with a broken glass bottle.

The officers raise their guns at Nowell, yelling at him to put the bottle down and to raise his hands. Nowell drops the broken bottle to the ground, causing it to break into more pieces. He then raises his hands up and gets on the ground on his knees. The officers approach Nowell and Elisha, one of them putting handcuffs on Nowell, the other two making sure Elisha is okay. The officer with the handcuffs tells Nowell that he is under arrest. He helps Nowell get to his feet, and all five of them go inside the Rivers Police Department.

25

A NIGHTMARE

Annalisa watches the news on the television in her office. Out of curiosity, she looked up 'Rivers USA news' online and has been reading headlines. She clicked on a video and is now streaming the Rivers Local News station to her television and is shocked. She sees that Elisha has been attacked by Nowell and that Nowell is now being held at the Rivers Police Department. It is rumored that Elisha is going to press charges for assault and that Nowell is under investigation for the death of Seth Thompson. Nowell's wife, Brianne Green, discovered Seth's body after leaving the Rivers Police Department to bring awareness to the death of Bridgette Miller, mother to Seth's son. After informing her husband of what she found, Brianne was on her way back to the police department while the assault took place.

"What a nightmare," Annalisa says to herself. She takes her phone out and dials a number. "Hello, Terry? The members of A Taste of Tongue are due any minute, right? Okay, well I need you to make sure they spend as little time as possible on their devices. I'm talking phones, TV, computers, you name it. They're from a college town in The States, and it is not looking good there, right now. I need the boys to not be distracted while they're here to handle their business. Send them straight to me when they arrive. Thank you."

Annalisa hangs up and continues watching the television for a few more moments, then turns it off in disgust. The timing couldn't be worse for a controversy involving Toby's parents to arise. Annalisa only hopes that whatever happens in Rivers does not make too much headway here.

A knock on the door soon comes. Terry, a balding middle-aged man, comes into the room and announces that A Taste of Tongue is with him. Annalisa tells him to bring them in, and Terry steps out the door. A few seconds later, Toby, Chris, and Eric come into Annalisa's office.

"Hello, there, boys," Annalisa exclaims. She meets the boys halfway and shakes their hands. "How was the flight?" The boys all nod and say the flight was good. "And your stay last night? I hope you three have been comfortable."

"Everything's nice, thank you," Toby says, confidently. "It's nice to finally meet you, Annalisa." He gestures to Chris and Eric. "These guys don't know you, though."

"Oh, I'm sorry," Annalisa says, eyes widening from embarrassment. "Annalisa Smith, CEO of Svelte Records. I've been watching your band for so long that I feel that I've already met you."

"Thanks," Eric says. "Hopefully, we'll all get to know each other very well."

Annalisa smiles. "That's the spirit! Now, I don't want to waste your time, so I'll get straight to the point. As you already know, the tour you guys set out on must start here in England since that's where the label is based. I'm thinking we can do a surprise show in London two days from now."

"A surprise show?" Toby asks. "What about a lead single or something like that?"

"You'll debut the new single at the surprise show. You guys can play whatever you want, but the second song in the set must be the single."

"Why the second song?" Chris asks.

"You attract fans by playing something familiar. Then you immediately catch them off-guard and hold their attention with an awesome new song. You guys up for that?'

The boys agree.

"Alright," Annalisa says, "let's talk about strategy."

NOWELL IS SITTING ALONE in the singular holding cell in the Rivers Police Department. An officer comes by and unlocks the cell, Elisha stepping inside. The officer tells Elisha to holler if anything funny happens and walks away after closing the cell door. Elisha, his face patched up after being struck by the bottle, looks at Nowell.

"I want you to know that I won't be pressing charges," Elisha says. "You may be a loud and violent asshole, but you're still my friend."

"Thank you," Nowell says calmly. He stares at Elisha's warm eyes, hoping to pierce them with the coldness of his own. "Now tell me what you really want."

"I want you, of course," Elisha says. He leans back onto the cell door, watching Nowell with pity. "What happened to us, Nowell?"

"Nothing happened to us," Nowell says. "We've just gotten older, that's all."

"We're still plenty young. There's so much life left in us both."

"Maybe not. They think I have something to do with

Seth's accident, but once they find out it's you, your life is over."

"That's where you're wrong, Nowell," Elisha says. He walks closer to Nowell and begins to whisper. "I paid someone to disable the cameras at your house. No one saw anything, and no one will see anything."

"So, is that why you talked to Janie? To frame me for something I didn't do?"

Elisha shakes his head and crosses his arm. "Janie and I care about you very much, Nowell. I took Bridgette and Seth out of the picture so you can have fewer counterarguments."

"Counterarguments for what?"

"For you to finally have the freedom that *you* seek. Janie and I have found your ticket out, and even though going about it won't be perfect, I assure you that you'll get the life, and the happiness, that you've always wanted."

Nowell sighs. "How are you going to do that?"

"Easily."

BRIANNE IS CRYING on the couch at home. The deaths of Bridgette and Seth, Nowell attacking Elisha, and the constant threat of her life taking a turn for the worst is becoming too much for her. She sees on her phone that it is rumored that Elisha will press charges after Nowell's attack, but she hasn't heard anything remotely concrete.

Brianne has the two children upstairs taking a nap as she feels sorry for herself drinking wine. She refused to step foot back into the house until Seth's body was removed by the Kingfish Funeral Home in Rivers. She couldn't risk having the children see Seth again, and she also thought she couldn't handle it herself. The sadness she feels makes her believe that the wine isn't helping, but she continues to drink anyway. After taking another sip from the glass, the doorbell rings. Slowly, Brianne gets up from the couch and walks over to the front door to open it. Outside the front door is Janie.

"Are you Brianne Green," Janie asks coolly.

Brianne takes a sip from her wine glass. "Sorry, ma'am, but I don't do auto— Wait a minute"—she squints at Janie—"I know you. I don't remember where from, though."

Janie nods. "Yes, you do know me. Just like I know you're Brianne Green. I was trying to play it cool since I figured you forgot who I was."

Brianne shakes her head. "No, I remember you. You saved me and my husband when we crashed our boat a few years ago." She takes another sip. "What's your name, what's your name?" She snaps her fingers and then points. "Jennifer?"

"No, but close. It's Janie."

"Janie...So, what brings you here?"

Janie gestures toward the inside of the house. "May I come inside? I might be here for a while."

Brianne nods. "Absolutely." She steps aside and lets Janie in, closing the door behind her. She walks past Janie and toward the kitchen. "Would you like anything to eat or drink?"

"No, thank you," Janie says. She sits on the couch, and Brianne comes over to join her. "I'm sorry to be the bearer of bad news, Brianne, but I'm here to tell you that your husband is not the type of man that you think he is."

Brianne stares at Janie with her red eyes. "Why do you say that?" She takes a sip of wine. "Nowell told me you raped him."

Janie scoffs. "He what?"

"You heard me. He told me that you raped him, and now we're watching your goddamn baby because of your lie."

"No, Brianne. You're watching my goddamn baby because of *his* lie. Just like how he lied to get you to lie alongside him on television. Well," Janie pauses, breaking eye contact, "I guess it wasn't a total lie on TV. He *did* cheat on you with me the night of the crash."

"Bullshit," Brianne says.

Janie shakes her head. "I promise, Brianne, it's not. The truth is, I've known Nowell for a very long time, and let me be the first to tell you that he is *not* a good person. He has no respect for women and only cares about himself."

"That's not true."

"It is true, Brianne," Janie says, her eyes filled with sympathy. "Deep down you know it is. And I'm going to tell you my side of the story."

26

F.E.E.L.I.N.G.C.A.L.L.E.D.L.O.V.E

"I don't think you want to listen to that."

It's 1993, and Janie is in a record store. She's browsing, flipping her fingers through the music until this voice speaks to her. She looks up and in front of her is Nowell in a different aisle.

"Oh yeah," Janie says, "and why's that?"

Nowell walks around to where Janie is, dragging his index finger across the top of the records. "Because those guys are too grungy, whining about their suburban lives and how average they have it." He makes it to Janie's side. "You need something lighter, poppier." He grabs a record two containers down from Janie and hands her the record. "I think *this* will suit you nicely."

Janie takes the record and looks at it. "Septua...Sep." She sighs. "I can't pronounce this, dude."

"It's Septuagenarian," Nowell says. "It means it's someone in their seventies."

Janie observes the album cover. "These guys look like they're maybe twenty-five."

"They have a gimmick," Nowell says. "The band wants to

release seventy albums before they make it to their eighties."

"How many albums do they have?"

"About thirteen. They've been pretty consistent, so far. I hope we all live long enough to see it through."

"So, you think these experimental weirdos are right up my alley?" Janie asks.

Nowell nods. "Yep. Trust me, when I first heard these guys, they blew my mind."

Janie tries to put the record back. "I think I'll pass."

Nowell, with a confused look on his face, stops her by lightly grabbing her arm. "Wait, what are you doing?"

"Putting it back," Janie says. She yanks her arm out of Nowell's grasp. "Let go of me, weirdo."

"I'm sorry," Nowell says, raising his hands in peace. He becomes a little excited. "Oh, I know! How about I buy it for you?"

Janie squints at him. "Buy it for me? Who even are you?"

"Oh, I'm sorry," Nowell says. He extends his hand and smiles. "Nowell Lewis."

Janie reluctantly shakes Nowell's hand. "Janie Smith."

Nowell nods. "Alright, Janie Smith. I'll buy this album for you, and then we can go listen to it together."

"Listen to it where?"

"Your place, my place. It doesn't matter."

Janie scoffs. "You're joking." She begins to walk away, but Nowell stops her.

"I promise," Nowell says, raising his right hand, "right hand to God, I won't do anything funny. I just want to share some music with you."

Janie takes a step back. "How old are you, Nowell?"

"I'm eighteen. You?"

"Seventeen. We can't go to my place because I still live with my parents."

"Then my place," Nowell says. "If your folks aren't expecting you back soon, we can knock this album out. It's only about forty minutes. What do you say?"

Janie crosses her arms, record still in hand, and mulls it over. She sighs. "Sure. What the hell."

Nowell smiles and puts his hands in a prayer position. "Awesome. Thank you." He takes the record from Janie. "You won't regret this, I promise." He nods his head toward the register up front. "Let's go check this bad boy out."

After purchasing the record, Nowell and Janie walk a few blocks to Nowell's house. It's an average-sized house that looks a little beat down on the outside. Nowell unlocks the front door, and the two go in.

After closing the door, Nowell says "Make yourself comfortable. I live here alone, so don't be afraid to be yourself or whatever."

Janie walks to the kitchen. "Be myself?" she asks, leaning on the counter as Nowell goes to his bedroom. "You just met me thirty minutes ago. What do you mean 'be yourself?'"

Nowell comes into the living room, which is connected to the kitchen. He's changed into a white T-shirt and shorts. "Just be yourself. Tell me about yourself." He walks into the kitchen with Janie and goes to the cupboard. "Do you want anything to drink?"

"Um, yeah. Water."

Nowell pours two glasses of water and hands one over to Janie, who thanks him. "So," Nowell says, "ready to give Septuagenarian a listen?" He walks into the living room and starts to put on the record.

Janie follows him. "How do you pronounce that so easily?" She sits on the couch.

Nowell drops the needle on the record and sits with Janie. "I told you. These guys blew my mind when I first listened to them. Let's listen."

The music begins to play, and the room is filled with new-wave music the likes of which Janie's never heard. She can feel the bass through her feet on the floor, the sound of the drums pulsates in her ears, and the guitars make Janie nostalgic for a childhood she's never had. Before she knows it, the first side is over, and she's sitting on the edge of the couch, tears going down her face.

Nowell sits up. "So, what do you think?" He sees Janie's face. "Are you okay?" He puts his glass on the table in front of them and lightly turns Janie's face toward him. "Janie, what's wrong?"

"I..." She clears her throat. "I'm sorry." She laughs half-heartedly and looks away from Nowell. "I don't know what came over me," she says as she looks back at Nowell.

"It's amazing, right?" Nowell wipes away her tears.

"Thank you," Janie says. "Um, can we listen to the other half?"

"Yeah, yeah," Nowell says. He gets up and flips the record over. The music starts once he sits down. By the time side B is over, Janie and Nowell are kissing each other passionately.

Janie notices the label on the record popping over and over and tries to pull away. Nowell stops her and grabs her breast. "Stop," Janie says.

Nowell pulls away, taking his hand off her. He clears his throat. "Sorry."

"It's okay," Janie says. She stands and straightens her skirt. "Thank you for showing me these guys. I should probably get home."

Nowell leans back on the couch. "Where do you live? I can drive you."

"It's fine, but thank you."

Nowell points at Janie. "You've never been touched like that before, have you?"

Janie laughs nervously. "What?"

Nowell smiles and stands. "I'm sorry if I caught you off-guard."

Janie shakes her head. "No. Um, no, you didn't." She crosses her arms.

"So, you *have* had someone touch your boob before?"

"Why are you asking me this?"

"We're both young, Janie. It's a simple question."

After a pause, Janie shakes her head no. "That was my first time kissing someone, too."

Nowell tilts his head, intrigued. "Really? I hope you weren't overwhelmed. You were excellent."

"Thank you," Janie says, trying not to smile. "I, um, I don't have class tomorrow. I can call my parents and tell them I'm spending the night at a friend's. If you still want to hang out?"

Nowell nods excitedly. "Yeah, absolutely. Um, just to get this out the way, I do have plans with my friend Elisha in the morning. So, if you wake up and I'm not here— Oh wait." He goes into the kitchen and grabs a notebook and a pen. He writes something down and tears off a sheet of paper. He returns to Janie. "Here's my number. If I'm not here in the morning, just give me a call sometime."

Janie takes the sheet of paper and puts it on the table. "Thank you. I'm gonna call my parents real quick, and we can hang out some more, okay?"

Nowell nods and says, "Yeah," quietly.

After stepping outside and calling her parents, Janie

comes back in and sees Nowell on the couch with a glass of bourbon in his hand. She comes and sits beside him.

"You wanna pick up where we left off?" Nowell asks. He takes a sip and hands the glass to Janie. She drinks from the glass and coughs a little.

"Where exactly?"

Nowell takes the glass from her and puts it on the table and embraces her. The two of them spend some time on the couch before going into Nowell's bedroom, where they got to know each other.

This is how Nowell and Janie spent their time together for the next year or so. Janie graduates high school in 1994 and moves in with Nowell. Before she moved in, Janie would talk with Nowell about music and pop culture before the two of them proceeded to Nowell's bedroom. After she moved in, Janie and Nowell hardly ever talked unless it was asking the other what they wanted to eat or what position they'd like to be in. None of this bothered Janie, not even Nowell gradually using protection less and less until the time came when he wasn't. Janie was content that she had found someone who she felt close with and so intimately entwined.

So, it broke her heart how Nowell reacted when she told him she was pregnant.

"You're fucking joking, right?"

The two are in the kitchen, sitting at the table. Nowell stares at her intensely, and Janie awkwardly adjusts in her seat.

"I'm not joking," Janie says. "I've missed two periods."

"Oh, wow." Nowell takes a sip from a beer can. "I thought you were on the pill?"

"I've never said that."

"You know, I just assumed you were, considering what we've been doing."

"Well, I'm not, and you probably should've asked before you started doing what you were doing."

"Me?" Nowell asks, leaning closer. "I think we're both equally responsible, here."

"Look, Nowell," Janie says, "we need to start planning what to do here."

"What is there to plan? I'll schedule an appointment for you to get rid of it."

"Get rid of it? You don't even want to talk about it first?"

"That's what we're doing right now," Nowell says, grabbing his beer. "We fucked up, and now you're pregnant. We're both young, so we get you an abortion." He takes a sip from his beer can.

"Well," Janie says, "I want to keep it."

Nowell puts the can down. "Well, I don't. Look, Elisha has more than enough money for us to use to go get you one. We can have this done this week."

"I don't want that, Nowell."

"Well, I don't want a kid yet, Janie. I'm fucking nineteen years old. I have— we have our whole lives ahead of us."

Janie leans back in her chair and crosses her arms. "I'm keeping it, whether you like it or not. I have a family in England that will help me take care of the baby, if you won't."

Nowell looks at Janie for a few moments, then throws the beer can across the house. Janie screams, and Nowell advances toward her, his finger in her face. "Listen here, you fucking bitch. That baby is as much as mine as it is yours, and I deserve to have a say in this matter."

Janie tries to push Nowell away. "Leave me alone," she says, crying. Nowell slaps her and points again.

"No," he says. "If you want to keep the damn thing, then fine. I won't stop you. After it's born, though, I want nothing to do with it. You have your rich Catholic fucks for relatives in England? *They'll* help you after I make sure the damn thing is healthy. Do you understand?

Janie nods, sobbing.

"Elisha and I will keep tabs on you. If you *ever* try to contact me again once I leave, we will fucking kill you. I don't know how, but I swear on my life that I will end yours." He sits back down. "I'm gonna let you stay here, for the time being. But I'll be going over to Elisha's and dealing with business with him until you're ready to go over to England. I'll see if he can set up his headquarters for Svelte over there."

"What is wrong with you?" Janie asks.

Nowell shakes his head. "Nothing's wrong with me." He puts his index finger on the table. "I'm doing whatever I can to survive and be happy in this country. If you want to ruin *both* our lives by having this baby now, then I'll make damn sure that you will have the most difficult time trying." He gets out of his chair and walks to the front door. "Call me whenever you're ready to move. Elisha and I will be ready." He opens the door but stops. "Also, you might want to get checked. I've been with Elisha this entire time. *That's* someone who knows how to make a man happy."

Janie begins to sob harder, and Nowell walks out the door, slamming it.

27

SIFTING

In the present, Elisha gets the cops at the Rivers Police Department to let Nowell go. After making it clear to the policemen that no more wrongdoing will occur, Nowell and Elisha exit the building and get into Elisha's car. After both doors are closed, Elisha speaks.

"You know *exactly* where that gun is in your house, correct?"

Nowell nods. "Exactly. We go to my house, you wait in the car, and I'll go upstairs to get it."

"What about Brianne," Elisha asks.

"What about Brianne?"

"What do you do if she's there? If she starts asking questions?"

"I'll tell her that I'm disposing of the gun before any policemen come over and find it. I'm simply getting rid of it —that way we're not even greater subjects."

"So neither of you are blamed for Bridgette's death, thus potentially leading to Seth's," Elisha says.

"Yes."

Elisha cranks the car. "Perfect. Let's move on then." He

pulls out of the parking lot and begins to drive to Nowell's house. When they make it there, they both see Brianne's car out front. Elisha parks beside the vehicle and relaxes in his seat. Nowell unbuckles his seat belt.

"This should only take a few minutes," Nowell says. "If I'm not out soon then come get me."

Elisha shakes his head. "No. I don't think she should know I'm here, let alone see me."

"You'll be okay. If you didn't want her to know you were here, then we shouldn't have taken your vehicle." Nowell opens his door. "I'll be right out."

Elisha sighs and nods.

Nowell gets out of the car and closes the door. He walks up to the front door of the house and walks in. "Bri, I'm home!" Nowell comes inside the house and sees Janie and Brianne sitting on the couch, staring at him. He slowly closes the door, facing the two women the entire time. "What's going on here?"

Brianne, tears in her eyes, exclaims, "You monster! You dirty, lying monster!"

Nowell raises a hand and takes a step closer. "Calm down, Bri. What's going on?"

"Don't tell me to calm down! How could you keep this secret from me?"

"Brianne, what are you talking about?"

Brianne points at Janie. "She told me everything, Nowell. I trusted you and have stood by your side through all the controversy. But you're just a lying snake."

Nowell lowers his hand. "Whatever it is she told you, you're just gonna trust her? That doesn't seem rational, don't you think?"

"Oh, don't you talk about rationality, you sexist prick. I feel it in my soul that she's telling the truth."

Nowell laughs to himself. "In your soul, Brianne? In your fucking soul? You hardly even know this woman, this liar who has come into our home and has tried to ruin our life, and you choose to trust her because of your silly little soul? Are you *actually* that goddamn dense?"

"I loved you, Nowell," Brianne says. "You could've told me this from the beginning, and I would have supported you no matter what. But, years of keeping secrets and lying is unforgivable."

"Unforgivable? What are you gonna do, punish me?"

"I'm leaving you, Nowell," Brianne says, sniffling. "Janie and I are going to go to the media and expose you. Your legacy will be tarnished, and any memory of you will be soured."

Nowell aggressively shakes his hands and head. "No, no, no. You two are not doing *any*thing." He takes a couple of steps closer. "What we're *all* going to do is sit down and talk about this like adults. None of the crying and lies about our past bullshit. We're just gonna talk this out."

Brianne stands, her hands in fists. "No! I've had enough of you. You will finally pay for all the wrong you've done. You have abandoned Janie, you have abandoned your daughter, and you've aided me in abandoning Toby. But you will *not* abandon me and that boy upstairs. We are leaving *you* behind, so you can finally know how it feels to the fullest effect. It's over, Nowell."

Nowell scoffs. "Fuck this." He walks forward and heads for the stairs. Brianne stands in front of the stairway, blocking him. "Brianne, get out of my way."

"No. Leave this house."

"I am leaving, you stupid bitch! Now let me go upstairs, so I can get some clothes and get out of your life."

Janie shakes her head while still on the couch. "Don't

listen to him, Brianne. Those boys are still upstairs. He'll just take them."

"Shut up!" Nowell yells. He looks back at Brianne. "If you don't let me upstairs, I *will* hurt you. Do you understand?"

Brianne spits in Nowell's eye, and after yelling in shock, Nowell pushes her into the wall. Brianne yelps as her back hits the wall hard, and she slides to the ground. Janie gets up quickly and runs over to Brianne to check on her. Brianne waves with a "Go" to Janie as Nowell begins to walk up the stairs, but Janie grabs the back of his shirt.

"Get back here, you coward!" Janie exclaims.

Nowell turns around and punches Janie in the face, and she falls to the floor. He makes it to the top of the stairs and looks over to see his son looking at him through the open doorway that was Toby's room. Nowell pauses for a moment before heading into his bedroom. He goes into the bathroom and grabs a step stool. He brings the step stool to the closet, opens the closet door, and gets on the step stool. On the top shelf in the closet is the brown bag that Richard gave to Toby years ago. Nowell grabs the bag with the gun inside and goes back down the stairs. Janie isn't in the living room anymore, but Brianne is in her exact same spot on the floor. She notices Nowell and looks up at him.

"I don't understand," Brianne says.

"Understand what?" Nowell asks.

"Anything that's going on. This city was supposed to be good for us. *All* of us. I just...don't understand."

"What's to understand?" Nowell says. With the gun still in the bag, but the opening of the barrel sticking out, Nowell pulls the trigger and shoots Brianne in the head. Janie appears at the doorway of the kitchen, holding a first-aid kit. She sees what Nowell has done, drops the kit, and runs toward the door. Nowell points the gun at her and shoots her twice in the back, and she falls to the ground, her head hitting the doorknob.

Nowell holds the bag to his side, breathing heavily and staring at Janie's body. A few moments later, Elisha opens the front door, struggling at first because of Janie. He looks down at her body, then looks over at Brianne's, with Nowell standing over it. Elisha makes eye contact with Nowell and walks over to him. They put their foreheads on one another, eyes closed, until Nowell's breathing becomes normal.

"Where are the boys?" Elisha asks, eyes still closed.

"Upstairs, to the right."

"Do you want to get them, or do you want me to?"

"You can go upstairs and grab them," Nowell says. "I'll step outside and call Richard."

"Okay."

The two open their eyes, Elisha beginning to go up the stairs and Nowell heading toward the door. Nowell stops and turns around. "Elisha," he says."

Elisha looks to Nowell. "What is it?"

"Cover their eyes." Nowell waves the gun in a circle. "They're too young to see this stuff."

"They'll be older after tonight," Elisha says, and he continues up the stairs.

28

STILL ILL

Nowell and Elisha met for the first time in 1987. On the first day of class, in 7th grade, they met in Mrs. Waterston's English class. Nowell and Elisha sat side by side at their desks and did not initially take notice of each other, even when Mrs. Waterston took roll and called their names. Not until lunch break later that day. Nowell had lived in Paleview all his life, but Elisha and his family were new in town. During their lunch break that day, some of the other classmates confronted Elisha and asked him many questions about his life. Questions like where he was from, was that his real name, and why was his hair so funny. Many questions that Nowell did not hear since he was on the other side of the quad, while Elisha and the group of boys were under the tree that stood proudly in the middle. It was impossible to not notice the group of boys under the tree and the group slowly grew. Nowell walked over to the group of boys to see what the fuss was about.

"The fuck do you want, Lewis?" one of the boys asks Nowell.

"I was just wondering what was going on over here."

"We got a new kid," the boy says. "We're just getting to know him."

Nowell raises an eyebrow. "Getting to know him?"

"Yeah." The boy walks over to Nowell and pushes him. "Is that a problem?"

Nowell stands silently for a few moments, looking down at his chest where the boy pushed him. Nowell then makes eye contact with the boy and punches him in the face. Most of the other boys see this and begin exclaiming and huddling around Nowell and the bully as they fight. After about a minute, a teacher runs over and breaks the two up. With bloody noses, Nowell and the bully are sent to the principal's office, who promptly suspends the boys from school. After classes that day, Elisha confronts Nowell at the front doors of the school.

"Thank you," Elisha says, "for beating that guy up."

"Butch had it coming to him, anyway," Nowell says, grinning. "So, what's your name?"

"Elisha."

Nowell nods. "Nowell. Nowell Lewis. What brings your family to Paleview?" he asks as the two of them walk down the sidewalk away from the school.

Elisha shrugs. "My dad is a construction worker. He found a job here."

"That's cool. Hey, are you in a rush to get home?"

Elisha shakes his head. "No. Why?"

"I like to hang out under the bridge downtown. You wanna go with me?"

"The bridge with the train track under it," Elisha asks.

Nowell nods. "Don't worry. I'll make sure you won't get hit."

Elisha reluctantly agrees, and the boys head to the train track. Once there, Nowell sits down with his back on the wall and takes a notebook out of his backpack. Elisha stands beside him, looking down. "What's that?"

Nowell, who has a pen out, looks up at Elisha. "Oh, I just like to write stuff."

Elisha sits beside Nowell and tries to look in the notebook. "What kind of stuff?"

"You know. Stories, poems, stuff."

"Can I see?" Elisha asks.

"Um, yeah. Sure." Nowell hands Elisha the notebook. Elisha goes to the front page and starts skimming each and every one.

"This stuff is pretty interesting."

"Thanks," Nowell says. "Why do you care?"

Still looking in the notebook, Elisha says, "I don't know. I've just always been into creative-type stuff. My dad doesn't like it because he says you can't make any money off it. But, I tell him that his job is creative, too. Just in a different way."

"Do you write or anything?"

"No," Elisha says. "I do have a keyboard that my parents gave me that I mess around with. I really like music."

"What kind of music?" Nowell asks.

"All kinds. Whatever catches my ear."

"Do you wanna make music when you grow up?"

"Maybe," Elisha says. He passes the notebook back to Nowell. "I haven't really thought about it too much."

"You should go for it, man," Nowell says. "You can make a boatload of money from making music. What you should do is be a producer. A lot of the money, but you keep the privacy."

"Yeah, maybe."

"Can we go to your house?" Nowell asks. "To see your keyboard?"

Elisha looks over at Nowell. "Are you serious?"

Nowell nods. "Yeah, man. Let me hear what you got."

Still caught off guard, Elisha takes a moment to agree. They then get up and head over to Elisha's house, the first time out of hundreds.

One time, in 1991, Nowell and Elisha were walking to Elisha's house only to see Butch and a couple of his cronies standing at the front door.

"Oh shit," Elisha says, beginning to turn away.

Nowell grabs Elisha's jacket arm. "Be cool, we got this." He nods toward Butch. "For what do we owe the pleasure of this visit?"

"Can it, Lewis!" Butch snaps. "You know goddamn well why we're here."

"Butch," Nowell says, "I told you I didn't mean it. Those eggs just happened to fall on your head, that's all. How was I supposed to know that you would be directly below me?"

"Do you think I'm dumb enough to believe that the day after I tagged the lockers of you two faggots saying that you suck eggs that it's a coincidence that this happened?"

"I honestly do, Butch, yeah," Nowell says.

"That's it," Butch says. He looks over at his entourage, and they all nod. He looks back at Nowell and Elisha. "We're gonna give you two a pounding you'll never forget."

"Shit, run!" Elisha exclaims, and he and Nowell turn and run away, Butch and his entourage following them. Nowell and Elisha run through the neighborhood, then through downtown, zipping and bobbing past people. They go into a vintage clothing store and hide in the back in a changing room, breathing loudly and trying not to laugh. Elisha sees the bullies come in, asking around if anyone saw Nowell and Elisha enter the store. One customer says that they saw someone run to the back. Before the bullies can investigate, Nowell and Elisha sneak out of the changing room. They make it to the front of the store and run to the bridge, hiding by the train track, the horn of a train in the distance.

"Do you think we lost them?" Nowell asks, panting. He leans over, his hands on his knees.

Elisha is standing with his back leaning on the wall. Also panting, he says, "Yeah, I think so."

After a few moments, Nowell straightens himself up. He walks over to Elisha and places his forehead on Elisha's. Eventually, Elisha's breathing goes back to normal, and the two laugh. Nowell places his hand on Elisha's cheek, and they look up at each other. The train passes by them, and the two share a kiss until the train is gone.

After their kiss, Elisha looks at Nowell. "Why did you do that?"

"You're my best friend," Nowell says. "It felt right to me." He takes a step back. "Did it feel right to you?"

Elisha looks at Nowell for a long time and says, "Everything feels right with you."

29

TWO OF US ON THE RUN

In the present, in Annalisa's office, the band members and Annalisa have just finished talking about their plan for the album launch. Annalisa closes a notebook and puts down a pen on her desk.

"Alright," she says. "Everything is in order now. Would you guys like to go get a bite to eat? My treat."

Chris stretches in his chair. "That sounds good. I'm starving."

"Same," Eric says. "What's there to eat around here?"

"Whatever you'd like, I'm sure we can find something for you," Annalisa says.

Toby stands from his chair and stretches. "Hey, where's the restroom around here?"

Annalisa points at her office door. "At the end of the hall you guys came through, turn right, and then turn left into another hallway. The restrooms are in that hall."

Toby gives her a thumbs-up, thanks her, and exits the office. He makes his way to the restroom and walks in. There are two men at the sink washing their hands.

"I mean it really is awful," one of the men says. "That poor town. And those poor kids."

"I wonder how long until they find out," the other man says.

"Find out what?" Toby asks.

The two men look over at Toby standing in front of the door. "Oh shit," the first man says. "Nothing, kid."

Toby raises an eyebrow. "Um, it didn't sound like nothing. What was that about a town and some kids?"

The two men look at each other then back at Toby. The second one sighs. "I won't go into specifics, but something has happened in your hometown."

"Where? Violet Valley?"

"No," the man says. "In Rivers."

"What happened in Rivers?" Toby asks.

"Joe, don't," the first man whispers to the other man.

"Look, kid," Joe says. "It's nothing major. Honestly."

Toby looks at the two men for a moment then down at his feet. "Hmm," he says to himself. He slowly turns away and exits the restroom.

"Goddammit," Joe says. He quickly grabs a paper towel and dries off his hands. "Hey, kid, wait!" The two men run out of the restroom, but Toby is already gone.

Toby walks into Annalisa's office. Chris, Eric, and Annalisa look over at him, smiling at first until they see Toby's face.

"What's wrong, dude?" Eric asks.

"Yeah, you okay?" Chris asks.

Toby walks over to the three of them and looks at Annalisa. "Annalisa, these two guys in the restroom just told me that something's wrong in Rivers."

"Is that so?" Annalisa says.

"Yeah," Toby says. "But they were acting all weird about it like it was a secret. What's up with that?"

"I, um," Annalisa begins, looking away for a moment.

The two men from the restroom come into the office in a hurry. "Annalisa," Joe exclaims, "Toby is coming to tell you something." Joe looks around the room and realizes his mistake.

Toby, Chris, and Eric look at Annalisa, waiting for a response. Annalisa stands there awkwardly, starting but never finishing several sentences. Finally, she decides to tell the truth.

"I don't know *all* of the details, but these two people, Bridgette and Seth, are dead."

"What the fuck?" Eric says quietly, almost to himself.

"And Nowell attacked Elisha with a broken glass bottle. Elisha might be pressing charges, but I don't know anything about that yet. The Rivers Police Department think Nowell has something to do with the deaths since Seth died from an overdose and Bridgette was shot."

"Oh my God," Chris says. He sits down and sinks into the chair like the life has left his body.

"Why didn't you tell us this?" Toby asks.

"I didn't want you guys to be distracted," Annalisa says. "I'm sorry."

"You're sorry?" Eric exclaims. "My brother is dead and our friend is, too. You didn't want to tell us, and all you can say is you're sorry?!"

"I know it wasn't the wisest decision," Annalisa begins, "but if you just give me a moment to explain."

"Get us out of here," Chris says, getting up from his seat. "We have to go back to Rivers and make sure everything is okay."

"No," Annalisa says. "Toby is the son of a possible

murderer. He cannot under any circumstances go to Rivers right now."

"Why the hell not?" Eric asks. "That's where we're from. Our families are there. This *directly* involves us."

"No, it doesn't," Annalisa says. "It involves your loved ones, yes. But not you three. If you care about your band, your future, you stay here and make a statement online."

"Fuck that, dude," Chris says. "If you won't help us, then we'll just fly ourselves back." He looks over at Toby and Eric. "Come on, guys."

Chris and Eric begin to walk toward the door of the office. They pass the two men before they realize that Toby is not following them. They turn around and look at Toby, who is still standing in the same spot.

"Toby," Eric says. "Are you coming or not?"

Toby hesitates. "I think what Annalisa is saying is a good idea."

"You what?" Eric asks.

"She's right. What's best for us right now is to just stay here and not get involved with the drama back home."

"You may just see it as drama," Eric says, "but our best friends are *dead* now, Toby. And your piece of shit father might have something to do with it."

"We can't keep delaying our happiness because of Rivers, guys," Toby says.

"We're not delaying our happiness, Toby," Chris says. "We're going home. If you don't like it, then fine. The band's over. Whatever contracts or agreements we've broken, we'll pay for it. Eric and I actually have souls."

Chris and Eric exit the office, slamming the door behind them. Toby and the two men look at Annalisa. "What now?" Toby asks.

Annalisa sighs. "We'll work something out."

. . .

ELISHA and Nowell pull up to the NA building in Streamsville. It's a little after midnight, and the only lights on are from Elisha's headlights and the car parked right beside them. Nowell takes off his seat belt and turns to look in the back seat. He looks at the two children sleeping in the back and sighs. He turns back around, and Elisha puts a hand on his shoulder.

"It's gonna be okay," Elisha says. "It's almost over."

"You sure we can't take both of them?"

"You know we can't," Elisha says. He takes his hand off Nowell's shoulder. "It's for the best."

Nowell sighs. "Okay. Let's get this over with." He steps out of the car and takes out Seth's son from the back seat. Both of the front doors of the other car open, and Abigail and Richard step out. Nowell walks over to them, holding the child.

"What took so long?" Richard asks.

"Did everything go okay?" Abigail asks.

"We took out Brianne and Janie," Nowell says quietly, to not wake the baby.

"Fuck," Richard says.

"Why the hell would you do that?" Abigail says.

"They were going to tell everyone everything," Nowell says. "They wouldn't listen to me."

"So, you fucking shot them?" Richard asks. "Am I gonna have to get rid of their bodies, or did you two idiots take care of that?"

"We left them, and it doesn't matter," Nowell says. "Here, take the baby so we can move on." He hands over the baby to Abigail, who begins to rock him. Richard grabs a duffle bag from inside the car and hands it over to Nowell.

"This should take care of everything you guys need," Richard says. "I would try to leave the country even quicker now that you guys killed those two women."

"Thanks," Nowell says. "So, where are you two headed?"

"You know we can't tell you that, and don't tell us where you're headed either," Abigail says. "Hopefully, this is the last time we see or hear from each other."

"Right," Nowell says, looking away briefly. "Thank you, guys. For all of this."

"Don't," Abigail says. "Have a good one, Nowell." She gets in the car with the baby, and Richard nods at Nowell before joining them. Nowell steps out of the way as they reverse and drive off. Elisha pops the trunk, and Nowell puts the duffle bag in before getting in the front seat.

"You ready?" Elisha asks.

Nowell looks out the window into the dark. "Yeah. Let's go."

30

CAVALRY CAPTAIN

Chris and Eric return to Rivers and head straight to Eric's house. Eric's parents are distraught and hug Eric as soon as he comes through the door, tears running down all three of their faces. Chris decides to give Eric and his family a moment and leaves to go to his home. When he gets there, his aunt is there talking to his mother in the living room. They sit Chris down and tell him that Richard has disappeared and left a large sum of money only for Chris. His aunt said that Chris could do whatever he wanted with the money since it was his. After spending the next few days at home, Chris decides to use the money to start over with Eric to make another band. After all the events in Rivers, the two of them decide they want to write music about real events that people could relate to. The two boys were welcomed back in Rivers with open arms for their selfless act.

Nowell and Elisha relocated to Canada and lived in a log cabin in the woods. They laid low until they both grew their facial hair out, and even then, they spent most of their time indoors. Elisha eventually began teaching at a nearby college as a music teacher, going by a different alias from one of the fake IDs Richard had given him. Nowell stayed at home and watched his son, spending his time playing and reading to him. The only time he ever went out alone was to get groceries, avoiding eye contact with people just in case someone recognized him.

Toby stayed in England with Annalisa, making A Taste of Tongue a solo project. After rewriting some of the songs, he released his debut album which was a critical and commercial success. He toured around the world for six months and was called the voice of a generation. After the tour, he settled in Paris with Annalisa who soon became pregnant. The two of them sat side by side on their bed, doctor results in hand, not knowing what to do.

The End

ACKNOWLEDGMENTS

First and foremost, as always, I'd like to thank my wife Mooni. Getting this book out was a bitch and she has been supportive the entire way and gave me the go ahead when I only had a very rough four chapters. She truly is ride or die. Next, I would like to thank my sister who funded the blurb and was also supportive in the early stages of writing the book. I want to thank Nichols for also reading and critiquing the very rough beginning stages of *A Symphony for None* back when it was called *Lonely Souls.* Thanks to my friend Shannon for just being cool. Thanks to my mom, Lacy, Nichols, Halie, my sister, Shannon, and Mooni for voting for the name of the book, which is awesome. Shout out to u/daveproclaimed for coming up with the title in the first place. Special thanks to Beverly for patiently and eagerly waiting for this book for damn near a year (I hope you liked it). And lastly I would like to thank my mom, sister, and Mooni again plus Michael for keeping me alive to see this through...

ABOUT THE AUTHOR

E.P. Lane is an official novelist who currently lives in Louisiana with his wife, infant daughter, two dogs, and two cats. This is E.P.'s third book and he hopes you enjoyed it, or else his English Degree from Louisiana Tech would be worthless. While you ruminate on that, he is already writing the rough draft for his next book. If you blink, you'll miss him, so please keep your eyes on him at all times.

If you made it this far, I am eternally grateful! When you have the time, please leave a review. Positive or negative I appreciate it. Whenever you're bored, check out what I'm up to at **lane writings.com**

ALSO BY E.P. LANE

Cupid Failed: Collection One

Cupid Failed: Collection Two

Coming Soon: *A Vampire Novella* (October 2023)